FIFTH SUN

Otha Foster

KDP

ISBN-13: 9781791946401
Cover design by:Blair Foster
Library of Congress Control Number: 2018675309
Printed in the United States of America

CONTENTS

CHAPTER 1

Bill Clark generally hated the stereotypes people believed about Texans, although he fit most of them. He wore boots and a Stetson cowboy hat, and had several belt buckles the size of hubcaps, but ironically he'd acquired all those accoutrements after he'd moved to New Mexico. He was tall and lanky; six two and 220 pounds. He still had his west Texas drawl, and was always "fixin'" to do something. Still, he resented that people thought of Texans in such narrow terms.

Another Texas trait was that he was raised to never whine to strangers about his personal problems. "Most folks have their own set of problems," his father had told him. "Don't saddle them with yours." Bill believed that to be true. It was not about being tough, but kind. He was not a John Wayne, but John Wayne was not John Wayne. He was Marion Morrison from Iowa. Not Davy Crockett. Still, Bill didn't think Marion Morrison had kept his problems to himself to be tough.

Dr. Sawyer, the lady therapist whose couch Bill found himself on was charging him a ridiculous amount of money to listen to his problems. He could tell she didn't like him right off the bat. He suspected she was a lesbian, not because she failed to succumb to his charms. Lots of women eluded his charms, but because of her haircut and shoes. Her clothes were typical of the region, everything straight out of the REI store in Albuquerque. She was wearing a lot of polyvinyl khaki, but she didn't really seem to be that outdoorsy. Her shoes were Birkenstock sandals. Okay, that's a stereotype, and Bill knew it, but he was pretty sure he was right about her.

"Tell me one of your earliest memories," she said.

"Why?" Bill asked.

She frowned. "Whatever brought you here to me is a problem you developed over time. You are paying me to help you see why you do what you do that you want to stop. We need to find out where it starts. Earliest memory seems like a good place to start."

"Don't you people believe that everything is connected to how often I was breast-fed, or how I was potty-trained. I don't remember any of that."

She took a sharp breath in through her nose and sighed as she exhaled. "Look Bill, I know you don't want to be here. Still, you told your wife you were willing to give it a try. You do want to save your marriage, right?"

Bill nodded. "So, tell me again why I'm coming to this session by myself," he asked.

"Why do you think?" Dr. Sawyer asked.

"I figured it was because it's all my damn fault."

She smirked. "Your honesty, Bill, does make this a lot easier. No, it's not about fault. You came to me with a problem. We need to figure out what it is. And you are not the only one in this relationship who needs the therapy. Still, I think everyone can benefit from therapy. I go to counseling myself."

"That's one of my problems with this," Bill said. "How do I know you aren't more messed up than I am?"

"You don't," she said, "but often kings got advice from their fools, because they knew their fools had a different perspective. That's all I'm here to provide. Let me try."

"I really don't remember much about my childhood," he said.

"Would you like to try some relaxation techniques?"

"You mean hypnosis?"

"No, just some relaxation techniques. Mindfulness."

"Like meditation."

"Actually, it is meditation."

Bill shook his head and said, "What the hell. I'll try it. I can't get into a lotus position though."

"Won't be necessary. Just close your eyes and get as comfortable as you can in your seat. We'll begin by learning some slow breathing exercises."

After a few minutes Bill was relaxed. The slow breathing cleared his head. He was aware of all the noise in the room, especially the scratching of the doctor's writing on her pad. Outside he heard the motor of an early model Volkswagen Beetle. He recognized the sound because he drove one from his junior year in high school until he graduated from college.

Bill's father had given him the small German car as a form of birth control. Prior to that Bill drove the family's Minivan. One night Bill was caught rounding second base and heading for third by Sheriff Ruly behind the church where Bill's father pastored. After he and the young lady quickly dressed the sheriff put the girl in the backseat of his car and escorted Bill back home. The sheriff informed Bill's dad what had happened, and after being grounded for three months Bill's father presented him with the keys to a Volkswagen beetle.

Copulation might've been possible in such a vehicle, but not without risk of injury. Bill found it was difficult to persuade a young girl of even the loosest morals to give it a try. It was not until college Bill lost his virginity, but it was in a cheap hotel room in the next county. Bill smiled at that memory. Maybe this was working.

"What are you remembering?" the doctor asked. He didn't want to tell that, so he went back further. He remembered a big event. Actually, he knew it was probably the event they were looking for.

"I was six years-old, sitting on the couch in nothing but my underpants. My sister was in her crib in the next room. We were watching one of those shows that showcased old monster movies. It always began with a trembling hand reaching out and opening a creaking door, and then it flashed scenes from various black and white horror films of the thirties. Elsa Lancaster as the 'Bride of Frankenstein' was hissing just as we heard a staccato of thumps and then a loud thud on the wooden front porch. My father was out of town and my mom, who would have been in her late twenties, looked just as frightened as I was."

"Why were you only in your underwear?" Dr. Sawyer asked, interrupting and frustrating Bill. What difference did it make?

"Because my mother wouldn't let me be totally naked," Bill said, a little testily. "It was hot in south Texas. I wouldn't have worn the underwear if my mother hadn't made me. We lived in the middle of nowhere. No one could see me. When I'm home now, I'm usually naked. Valerie isn't really comfortable with it, but I hate getting dressed. I wasn't abused sexually, if that is what you are thinking. That's not where this story is going."

"Of course," she said. "I'm sorry I interrupted. For the record, I don't like to wear clothes either. I'm naked as often as I can be in the summer. Not so much in the winter, though."

That was a little more information than Bill wanted, but he shrugged it off and continued. "Well, my mother stood and went to the front door. She flipped on the porch light and opened the door. Back then most people had yellow light bulbs to keep the bugs away, but it didn't seem to work. The glow filtering through the screen door made Mom look paler than maybe she really was, but I could see she was shocked by what she saw.

"I crawled up on my knees on the couch and pulled back

the curtains to see what had made the noise. Lying flat on her back was a naked Mexican girl. Her long black hair was fanned out behind her head. I had a little sister, so I knew girls didn't have penises, but I'd never seen naked breasts or pubic hair before.

"'Is she dead, Mama?' I asked.

"'I don't think so,' Mama said. 'Go get the water jar out of the refrigerator and bring it to me.'

"I didn't want to, but I knew this wasn't a time to argue. I could barely hold the big glass mayonnaise jar that we used to keep cold drinking water in, but I got it to her. Mama unlatched the screen door and walked out onto the wooden porch. I stood in the doorway and watched. I noticed the girl's feet were bleeding on the bottom.

"That my mother let me stand and stare at this naked girl spoke to how shook up she was. It was totally against her sense of propriety. I once walked in on her in the bathroom and she almost broke my hand trying to slam the door shut."

"This modesty you describe," Dr. Sawyer interrupted, again. "Was your mother religious?"

Bill thought this interruption was more relevant this time. "Yes, very. She thought being naked was a sin. I bet she didn't look at herself naked in the mirror. We never missed Sunday School or church."

"It would then seem a little against her nature to commit adultery and abandon her children."

Bill saw where she was going with this and said, with a touch of irony. "Are you saying that there is never any sexual scandal among the Christians?"

Dr. Sawyer smiled. "No, I'm afraid it's pretty common. We'll talk about this later, but please continue with your story."

"Okay, my mother knelt down by the girl. 'Honey,' she

said. 'Honey, are you okay?'

"The girl didn't respond. Mom dipped her fingers in the cold water and sprinkled a little on the girl's face. Suddenly, the girl gasped and opened her eyes. She jumped to her feet and looked at me wide-eyed, and then at my mother. She turned, jumped off the porch, and ran towards our front fence. She leapt over it like a deer, and we never saw her again.

"'Billy Ray, go put some shorts on,' Mom said. 'I have to call the sheriff.'

"When she told me to get shorts, I realized that I had been standing outside in my underwear and that girl had seen me. I blushed with shame and ran and put on my Buster Brown shorts.

"Forester, Texas didn't have any law enforcement. There were only twenty people living in the village limits. Most of the people who did business in the general store and post office were ranchers. The sheriff would have to come from the county seat, Faytonville, which was forty miles away.

"I was asleep on the couch when the sheriff came, so I missed the conversation between him and my mother. When I awoke the next morning, my mother told me she didn't know any more than she had the night before. She said the sheriff said it was probably just a 'wetback' girl that had been raped by someone.

"'What is 'raped?' I asked.

"She took in a deep breath and said, 'It sort of means that some man tried to love on her when she didn't want him to.'

"'Like when I kissed Margo on the playground at school?'

"Mom laughed. 'Not exactly. That was just you showing some innocent affection. This was a grown man trying to do more than just kiss her.'

"'Why wasn't she wearing any clothes?'

"'That man probably took her clothes off her so he could do some bad things.'

"At six, I didn't have the foggiest notion why some man would want to take her clothes off her, or what those bad things were, but I did know that I would be angry if someone tried to take my clothes off me."

"It was about a week after that event that my mother left, and Dad said she'd run off with another man. I never saw her again."

Bill had told that story quickly and now he was trembling and didn't know why.

Dr. Sawyer just stared at Bill in a long silence. Finally, she said, "That's an incredible story, but I don't understand your reaction to it. Why are you so shaken? It was a traumatic event, to be sure, but why do you think it has such a strong impact on you?"

Bill brought himself under control by taking a few deep breaths and then he said, "I – I don't know."

"This is just a suggestion, but I'm wondering if it's just what you remember. Perhaps more happened than you remember. It's easy to see why you would remember this and were able to share it, but you went over very quickly what happened after. I think you may be leaving something out."

Of course, he was. He knew he was. And he was aware that he didn't want to remember it. He was also aware that she was going to try to make him remember it.

Dr. Sawyer sat and stared at Bill silently. Finally, she said, "You say it was only a week after that incident your mother left?"

"No," Bill replied. "It seemed like a week, but I guess it could've been a year — or years. More things happened. I know they did. I don't remember, and I'm pretty sure I don't want to remember."

Dr. Sawyer made a few notes on a yellow pad, and then she looked up and spoke with some hesitation. "I am not a Freudian psychoanalyst. So, whatever your stereotype is in your mind, please understand that I don't connect everything to sex. However, I think the details you shared about the girl's nudity, your near nudity, and your mother's modesty are significant in some way. It may not be sexual, though it seems likely, but nudity represents vulnerability."

"If I'd suffered some kind of abuse wouldn't I'd be uncomfortable being naked — being vulnerable, as you say?"

"Not necessarily. If you had been exploited sexually, and don't take this wrong, it's very possible that you didn't find it unpleasant at the time. At such a young age you wouldn't have known that you were involved in something that was wrong. You very likely enjoyed how it felt, but as you grew older and more aware of the social taboos you repressed the memory."

"You said you liked being naked. Are you repressing something?"

Dr. Sawyer laughed. "It's always possible. But you're paying me to help you and not vice versa. So, we won't dwell on my problems."

Bill looked at the clock on the wall, and he knew time was about up. He stood and stretched. "I guess I'll spend the rest of this week obsessing about all this. I'm not sure this is helping."

"The definition of mental health is still somewhat elusive. Exploring repressed memories can be dangerous. I am trained to help you do this without harming you, but there are no guarantees that any of this will help. Still, in my experience, most people are better off facing the truth. Have you told this story to Valerie?"

Bill shrugged. "I've never told this story before to anyone."

Dr. Sawyer frowned. "Not even to your buddies growing

up. Having seen a naked girl would have been a story they'd want to hear, I would imagine."

Yes, they would have. Jimmy would have been aroused and would not have hesitated to share his condition with the rest of the gang. That would have been a good reason not to share the story, but Bill had shared more lurid stories than that. Bill was somewhat surprised himself for never telling anyone. "I suppose it was because the event was connected so close to my mother leaving me, that I didn't want to go near it," he said.

"I can see that, but maybe you should tell Valerie. She might have some insights that could be helpful."

"Alrighty then," Bill said, putting on his hat. "I'll tell her. See ya next week."

"Bring Valerie with you. I want to hear what she has to say."

CHAPTER 2

As promised, Bill shared the story with Valerie. She was completely stunned. "I can't believe you never told me about that."

"It didn't seem important; I'd never really thought about it."

Valerie shook her beautiful blonde head and stared at him with her piercing green eyes. "Bill, you're a newspaper reporter. How could you not be curious about what happened back then? It's totally against your nature. Why don't you do some research, and find out what happened? There has to be some record of that event. It might even lead you to your mother."

Bill nodded. He had already thought of that. "It happened nearly forty years ago. Do you think they kept that Sheriff's report?"

She shrugged. "How hard could it be to find out? Search the Internet. Make a few calls. Maybe there's a story there."

"Dr. Sawyer said we could work on it in her sessions. She didn't think my exploring it will help with our problem."

"She doesn't know you like I do. And besides, you need to know if your mother is still alive. You need to know what happened."

Bill was a reporter, but also the publisher, editor-in-chief, sales manager, and janitor at the newspaper they owned. Valerie retyped most of the copy to send to the printers and they delivered the paper to all the vending machines and stores in their small New Mexico village. A few youngsters did most of the home delivery. The Copper City Chronicle was a weekly paper that reported mainly on town council politics, births, deaths, marriages, and public intoxications. Often many of those elements were in the same story. It was hardly hard-hitting investigative journalism.

"It's not exactly a story for our readers," Bill said. "It's too old and it happened in south Texas."

"You've written freelance before. Maybe you could sell the story to a Texas rag."

Bill considered telling Valerie about the possible abuse and the dangers of exploring repressed memories, and that he was genuinely afraid, but he didn't want Valerie to know. He couldn't think of any rational fake excuses, so he had no other choice but make some effort to pursue it. Valerie would never let him blow it off. He both admired and resented her for that quality.

Bill went to his computer. First, he went to the Social Security website to find the record of his mother's death. He had no reason to believe his father had lied to him. Lying was a sin, wasn't it? Still, if he was going to pursue this story it would be good to know the date she died. He tried putting in her name as it was when she was married to his dad, and then her maiden name. Nothing from either. He tried the name his father had mentioned as the person his mother ran off with, but still nothing. He put all the names in a search engine, and there with were fifteen million hits. He searched a few pages and decided to give up. He was certain that she was dead, and there was no reason to waste any more time.

He tried to find phone numbers. According to Wikipedia, Forester still existed, but there was no information of any help. Bill doubted if Faytonville was going to be much better. He couldn't remember the exact date of the event, but when he called the Faytonville courthouse he was told, rather testily, that there was not any computerized data prior to the eighties. "If there is any information at all," the clerk told him, "It'll be in a box in the basement. The boxes are marked, but they are just piled on top of each other. If you want to come dig through them, you're welcome, but I ain't gonna do it."

Bill told Valerie and he hoped that would be the end of it, but he suspected it wouldn't.

"You have to go. Take a few days off and go check it out. I can handle things here."

"But it's a good ten-hour drive to Fayton County from here."

"Catch a jet in El Paso, fly to San Antonio, and rent a car," she said. "If you don't find anything, you can write a travel story so we can still write it off as a business expense."

Bill stared at her. She kept the books, and she wasn't usually so generous with the paper's money. "You sure seem anxious to get rid of me," he said.

"I'm not cheating on you, and if I was, I don't need to get rid of you to do it. You spend every waking hour here at the paper. I've got plenty of opportunities to cheat on you. I want you to find out what happened with that girl and your mother."

Nothing she said made Bill feel any better. He knew it was irrational, but he was terrified that if he left, he would come home to find her gone. Telling her what he felt would sound needy and obsessive, and it was just the kind of thing that put him into therapy in the first place. He went home to pack.

CHAPTER 3

Faytonville was fifty miles from San Antonio, but there wasn't an airport closer. Living in the mountains of New Mexico, Bill had forgotten how oppressive the heat could be in south Texas in June. He had the air conditioning going full blast in the little Honda Civic he'd rented, but he was still sweating.

Bill was sure he'd been to Faytonville, but he didn't remember. However, he had no trouble finding the courthouse. Like most small county seat towns in Texas, the courthouse was in the center of the town, and it looked like every other courthouse square in every other little town in Texas. The only thing different would be the names on war memorial out front. Another difference was the statue of the Col. Gayle Fayton who founded the town after fighting in the battle of San Jacinto. According to the plaque at the base of the statue, the brave future Confederate colonel missed the battle of the Alamo because of a drinking binge in New Orleans, but recovered to participate in the battle that won the war. Such are the heroes of Texas history.

When Bill entered the courthouse, things were so quiet he was wondering if anyone was there. All the doors to all the offices were closed. Black lettering on frosted glass doors told him the purpose of each office. The Clerk of Records was the man Bill wanted to see, so he went to that office and turned the worn brass doorknob. He entered a large musty smelling room with shelves and shelves of large green ledger books.

In the middle of the room was a green metal desk with a computer terminal. Typing with limp wrists at an amazing speed was a stern-looking gray-haired man staring at the monitor through half-moon glasses. Bill closed the door a little too loudly, so the man had to have known he was there, but he didn't look up. "Excuse me, Mr. Tremaine. I'm Bill Clark. We spoke on the phone."

"I know who you are, Mr. Clark," he said, without slowing down his typing. "I can't believe you came all the way down here from New Mexico just to complicate my life."

Why did they always hire people like this for these jobs? The clerk back home was an old lady with a croaking voice from years of smoking, but she had the same attitude. It was as if the world was going to end if one more person interrupted their important work. What did this guy really have to do that was so important? "I'm not trying to be trouble, but I could use your help," Bill replied.

"Well, you're going to be sorry." He stood, removed his glasses, and brushed past Bill. "Follow me," he said.

He led Bill across the hall and down some dusty unpainted concrete stairs into a dark basement. He yanked a chain, and a bare light bulb illuminated a large oak door. He unlocked the door and reached in and flipped a switch. A bank of fluorescent lights buzzed and blinked on. Bill saw rows and rows of cardboard file boxes piled five boxes high. There were thousands of them and none of them were on shelves.

"What you are looking for should be over in that corner," he said, pointing in a general direction. "The boxes are marked, but I can't promise they are in any special order. If you want something copied, you can bring it up to me and I'll copy it for you. Do not remove anything and make damn sure you put everything back the way you found it."

"Thank you," Bill said to the man's back as the man walked quickly back up the steps

It took Bill three hours of moving heavy boxes and working up quite a sweat, but he finally found the box he was looking for. Digging through it he found the original report of the incident made by the sheriff's deputy. Bill felt a little tinge of pride at the description that his mother had given the deputy. She described it with such great detail that he could see it clearly in his mind. She'd have been a good reporter. Bill took note of the date and the deputy's name, but there was nothing more than what he already knew—except for one thing. His mother had told the deputy that the girl had a small tattoo of a sun on her left shoulder.

Today, a tattoo on a young girl would be commonplace, especially sun tattoos, but back then tattoos were only on men who'd been in the military or were in motorcycle gangs. Most Mexican kids in south Texas were raised Catholic, and tattoos would have been considered a sin.

Bill sat on the floor with the open box, searching for any follow-up information, but there didn't seem to be any. Apparently, the deputy took his mother's statement and that was as far as it went. Suddenly a shadow darkened where he was working. Bill looked up expecting to see Mr. Tremaine, but instead he saw a large Latino man in a cowboy hat.

"What the hell are you doing?" he asked.

"Hi," Bill said. "I'm Bill Clark. I'm a reporter researching a story."

"You're not from our paper."

"No sir."

"We don't like outsiders diggin' around in our records."

Bill stood up and offered his hand, but the cowboy didn't take it. "And you are?" Bill asked.

"I'm Sheriff Enrique Guitierrez."

"Well, Sheriff, I'm sure you know that I have a right to access these records because of the Freedom of Information Act. I could get a court order, but I didn't think I would need to."

"And I could throw your ass in jail for trespassing."

Bill stepped back and said, rather timidly, "The clerk let me in here."

"Maybe he did and maybe he didn't, but that would depend on whether or not you want to make trouble. The judge is fishing in Galveston, so I could lock you up until he gets back."

Bill lived in New Mexico now, but he was born and raised Texan. Anyone who had studied Texas history knows that lawyers and court orders didn't build Texas. This state was built by tough no-nonsense men and women. People like this sheriff.

Bill believed in the power of the pen, but he would never pit it against a Colt .45, or as he observed in this instance, a Glock 9mm. "I don't want any trouble, Sheriff. Maybe I could explain--"

"I know why you are here, Mr. Clark, and I don't like it. My predecessor might not have done a good job, but I don't want some writer trying to get a Pulitzer trashing a Fayton County Sheriff, no matter how long ago. You may get a great story out of it, but when you start digging up mistakes from a past sheriff, people start looking at the current Sheriff. It was a long time ago. Leave it alone."

Bill could see that this man was genuinely upset. "This happened before you were even born. How could it affect you?" Bill asked

"Politicians are always looking for reasons to cut my funds," he said. "A frightened and naked (he pronounced it "nekkid.") Mexican girl neglected by someone in my office, no matter when it happened, will poison the water."

It was strange to hear his Texas twang and colloquialisms, and Bill wondered if he'd purposefully eliminated any hints of a Mexican accent. Things had changed, but Bill imagined it was still pretty tough for a person of Mexican descent to get elected Sheriff in that part of the state. Bill wondered if the man even spoke Spanish.

"So, you know the case?" Bill asked.

The sheriff frowned. "I believe you were leaving, Mr. Clark."

"I'll just clean up--"

"I'll get it," Guitierrez said. "Just go."

"You sure? That bitchy clerk was pretty insistent that I clean up."

"Get the hell out!"

As Bill left the courthouse, common sense told him he should point his car north and not look back. But now Bill wanted to know what the sheriff was afraid of. Bill wasn't going anywhere.

CHAPTER 4

Bill needed to find someone who would be more sympathetic. So far, Faytonville had been less than hospitable. Of course, Bill knew that small Texas towns often seem friendly on the surface, but they can always spot a stranger, and they tend to keep a close eye on him.

As Bill stood on the courthouse steps, he surveyed the businesses across the street, and he spotted what he was looking for. He read "Faytonville Gazette" in big gold letters across the big storefront window. If he were going to find a sympathizer, it would be there.

A bell tinkled as he opened the door. There was no one in sight. In the middle of the large room was a solitary desk with large computer monitor and keyboard. Filing cabinets lined one wall. On the desk was a wire inbox that was full to overflowing and a matching outbox that had a solitary sheet of paper in it. Bill smiled thinking that it looked just like his desk back home.

"I'll be right there" A woman's voice shouted from a back room. Bill heard a toilet flush and then a petite blonde entered from the back drying her hands with a paper towel.

She tossed the towel in the trash and offered Bill her hand, which was still a little damp. "What can I do for you?" she asked.

"I'm Bill Clark. I operate a newspaper in Copper City, New Mexico like your operation here, I imagine. I was hoping I might get some assistance from you on a story I'm working on."

She laughed, and Bill noticed the dimples in her cheeks and the sparkling brown eyes. Bill found her quite fetching.

"You must have a bigger operation than what I got if you have a travel budget," she said.

"We don't—I'm sorry, I didn't catch your name."

"That's because I didn't throw it. I'm Cathy Elkins, Bill," she said. "I'll help you if I can."

She pointed to a chair next to her desk. Bill sat down and crossed his legs. "I don't really have a travel budget, either, but this is kind of a unique situation. I'm researching a story about an event from my childhood. There may not even be a story, but I feel a need to satisfy my curiosity. I've been to the courthouse and was met with some resistance, which has piqued my curiosity further."

"You must mean Chuck Tremaine. He's the designated asshole of Fayton County, in more ways than one."

Bill chuckled. "You're fortunate if you only have the one, and I agree that he qualifies, but it was the sheriff that ran me out of the courthouse."

She frowned. "Ricky? Really? He's usually a pretty nice fella. That's not like him at all. Maybe you better tell me what you're looking for."

Bill quickly summarized the story of the girl on his porch. He left out the part regarding his mother's departure.

She smiled and nodded. "I've actually heard a version of that story before. It's attached to local legend, but I didn't think it was actually true. In the story she was murdered and haunts Forester as a ghost."

"She wasn't a ghost at the time it happened. I was six, so she seemed like a grown woman to me, but the deputy's report says my mother told him she thought she was about fourteen or fifteen."

"So, if she were still alive, she'd be in her fifties today." Cathy pulled out a legal pad and started making notes. She was taking Bill seriously. That was a good sign.

"I don't know what to look for at this point," Bill said, "but apparently there was no real investigation of the incident. The sheriff talks like I might be trying to cast aspersions on his office, but I suspect there is something else going on."

She looked at Bill pensively for a moment and said, "I suspect you might be correct, but his point is valid. People don't put stories from the past in context of the times. To blow off an investigation about a naked Mexican girl would have been the politically expedient thing to do at the time. No one wanted the sheriff's office wasting taxpayer money on a girl that probably wasn't even a citizen. And there was no real evidence of a crime. But such neglect today would bring in the ACLU and LULAC and probably the Texas Attorney General. Even though the story has nothing to do with Ricky's operation today he doesn't want them to start investigating him. Any publicity, even about something in the past, could draw unwanted attention by the legislature. Ricky could lose some of his state funding and eventually his job."

Bill nodded. "I understand all that and I know it to be true, but my gut says the sheriff is hiding something."

"What could he be hiding? He wasn't even born, yet."

"What about his family? Were any of them in law enforcement?"

"Ricky has never told me much about his family. They were probably illegal—pardon me-- I mean 'undocumented laborers.' He was born here, so he's a citizen. He told me once that his mother used to be a cook at the Blue Bonnet Café, but not anymore. Speaking of which, would you like to join me for lunch at the Blue Bonnet? Best chicken fried steak in the state."

"That is quite a claim," Bill said. "I imagine a lot of cafes in Texas would argue the point, but I certainly want to check it out. It won't cause a scandal, will it? I know how small towns talk."

"It might, but everyone here thinks I'm a slut anyway."

Bill's eyebrows shot up. "Really? Why is that?"

"Maybe it's because I'm thirty-two, divorced, and I've had sex with just about every man in this town."

Bill squirmed a little in his seat. "Relax," she said. "I'm just kidding. I am divorced, but I don't sleep around. I'm sure there will be some speculation about us. If you're afraid it'll get back to your wife, then we can forget it."

"I'm not worried. I think it could only improve my reputation," Bill said, laughing. "So, you don't think Ricky is involved in something that is connected to this story in some way?"

"I suppose he could be, but I don't know how. Sorry."

Bill sighed. "Well, that's okay, but I got to write something so I might as well go and do some research. Do you have an archive of the Gazette issues from that time period?"

"Not here, but they have it on microfiche at the library. It wasn't the Gazette back then. It was the Fayton Daily Sun. I changed the name when I bought it, because I knew I was going to make it a weekly paper."

"I understand. I had to do the same with my paper. Will the library have a computer I can use?"

"Yeah, but it's archaic and still on a dial-up modem. You can use mine, if you like. I'm on my way out. I have to go take some pictures of Ms. Lander's third grade class. They had perfect attendance."

"Been there, done that. Such a glamorous life we lead. I promise not to download any porn."

"I don't mind. Just don't delete any of mine," she said, laughing. "I get really bored sometimes. Just pull the door to when you leave. It'll lock by itself. I'll meet you at the Blue Bonnet, right over there." She pointed and I saw the small diner through the window. "The library is a couple of blocks over around the other corner."

Bill watched Cathy's behind as she walked out the front door. Her sway seemed a little exaggerated, which made Bill think she either knew, or expected him to look. Women who wear such tight jeans must have that expectation. His thoughts went to Valerie and he wondered if there was some sleaze back in Copper City staring at her behind.

CHAPTER 5

Against his better judgment, Bill pulled out his cell and called Valerie.

"How's it going?" she asked.

"Slow, but I think I might be onto something here. I got some resistance from the local law enforcement, but the local press is friendly."

"Friendly? Wait a minute--I know what you usually mean by friendly. You mean female and attractive, don't you?"

Bill chuckled nervously. "Yeah. Her name is Cathy. She and I have a date for lunch."

"Be careful, Bill. I'm checking out the copy machine repairman's butt as we speak."

Bill laughed. "Did he hear you? Tell Harold I said 'hi.'"

"He said he feels like he's just a piece of meat."

Harold was about five foot seven inches and two hundred and eighty pounds--a big piece of meat. "Well, try to keep your hands to yourself," I said.

"You do the same, buster," she replied. "Anything I can do on this end to help?"

"Nah, I'm going to the library to do some research, but I don't even know what I'm looking for."

"You'll know it when you see it. You've always been good at research."

"Yeah, but I really hate it. I'll call you again later this

evening. I love you."

She said, "Love you, too," and hung up. Bill checked his e-mails on Cathy's computer. All he had, as usual, was a few jokes from friends and multiple offers to increase the size of his penis or breasts. He wasn't too worried about his penis, and unfortunately his breasts were growing just fine without any help.

Bill did a web search on "sun tattoos," but found only pictures of the variety of sun tattoos available. He couldn't find a Wikipedia entry. There was nothing to suggest why a fourteen-year-old girl would have a sun tattoo back in the seventies. Actually, Bill discovered that tattoo parlors were blamed for a hepatitis epidemic in New York and that many of the present-day regulations were created back then, which would suggest a tattoo would have been considered a very bad idea for even a sailor, much less a young girl.

The Internet often makes research a lot easier, but for some things it wasn't very reliable. It was time to, as his nephew would say, "kick it old school." He headed for the library.

The library was a small brown brick building, newer than the other buildings surrounding it. Bill was struck by how clean the place smelled as he entered. There was no hint of the musty old books that most libraries have. That either meant they did something to actively remove that smell or they didn't have any musty old books.

"May I help you?" asked a pleasant-looking lady in her sixties, maybe early seventies, with beauty shop coiffed silver-gray hair. She didn't have reading glasses on a chain around her neck, but otherwise she fit the stereotype of what a librarian should look like. She reminded Bill a little of his maternal grandmother who died when he was thirteen.

"Yes ma'am, I would like to look at some microfiche of the newspaper."

She stared at Bill for an uncomfortably long time, and finally said, "You must be Mr. Clark. I'm Charlotte Brown. Cathy called me and told me you would be coming. I've already laid out some of the papers you might be interested in. I'll show you how it's catalogued, and you can help yourself to whatever else you might need."

"Did Cathy tell you what I was looking for?" Bill asked.

"Yes, she did." Charlotte said. "I think I found what you need."

"Were you here then, Charlotte? You remember anything about it?"

She hesitated for a moment and then said, "I'm lucky if I remember what I had for breakfast. I guess I was here back then, and I remember some gossip, but that's about it."

"Gossip? What about?"

Bill could tell that she wished she hadn't said what she had just said. She took a deep breath and said, "There was talk about the girl being pregnant by a much older man, but I'm sure that came out of nowhere. The newspaper stories didn't say anything about anything, and the sheriff's department didn't investigate anything, as far as I could tell. I think the gossip was just that."

As with the sheriff, Bill suspected Charlotte was hiding something. Maybe he was just being paranoid, and speaking of paranoia he wondered if Cathy was running interference for him to help him, or was she establishing a network of people to keep an eye on him? He was not being as irrational as one might think. He was a reporter. If another reporter came sniffing around his town, he'd want to know what he was up to every minute. Bill would bet good money that Charlotte would call Cathy the instant he left the library.

"Well, it's nice to meet you, Ms. Brown. Thank you for being so accommodating."

"Please call me Charlotte, and I am just doing my job."

"Thank you, Charlotte. Not everyone here shares your attitude."

"Yes, Cathy told me that your first impression of our village was Chuck Tremaine. I hope the rest of us can prove to you that we aren't all soreheads like Chuck."

"Well, if the rest of the people are as charming as you and Cathy I might just move here."

She laughed. "Let's not go overboard, Mr. Clark."

"It's Bill. You're right. That was laying it on a little thick."

Charlotte showed Bill everything he needed to know and soon he was skimming through the old Fayton Daily Sun's with ease. Bill hadn't used a microfiche reader in years, but the skill came back quickly.

As he scanned, he noticed Charlotte's reflection on the screen of the machine. Bill turned around and said, "I think I got it, Charlotte."

She didn't leave but stared intently at Bill.

"If you don't mind me asking, Bill, why are you doing this?"

"I don't mind you asking, but some of my reasons are personal, and I'd rather not talk about it."

Charlotte nodded. "Why have you taken so long? I mean, I don't want to pry, but it seems like if this was personal it would be important, and if it was important, you wouldn't have waited so long to look into it"

She sounded a little annoyed.

"To be honest, Charlotte, I don't know why it's taken me so long."

"We all have ghosts in our past, Bill. It's dangerous, I think, to go chasing after what haunts us. Some things in the past should probably stay in the past."

Bill looked up at her and noticed the intensity in her stare. What was she talking about? He just met this woman. Who the hell was she to tell him how to live his life? He started to tell her that, but he thought about it and figured he didn't need to make any more enemies than he had to. "Well, for me it's important to deal with my past to fix my future, but I suppose you could be right."

Her face softened and then she laughed. "Like most librarians I read too damn much, and ghost stories are my passion. I'm sorry for the dramatics. Still, I hope you don't do anything to harm one of our legends."

"I'm looking for two ghosts," Bill said, telling her more than he intended.

Again, with the intense stare. "What are you talking about?"

"I'll tell you what, Charlotte. I'll let you proofread my story before I print it. If you think it's going to do some harm, I'll just not print it."

She laughed. "You are a very good liar, Bill Clark."

CHAPTER 6

After ninety minutes of staring at microfiche, Bill still hadn't found anything significant and it was time to meet Cathy for lunch. He shut everything down, folded up his notebook, and thanked Charlotte for her help. He was running a little late, so he tried to jog a little bit, but quickly realized that wasn't such a great idea. He couldn't recall the last time he'd done any running, but he didn't think it had hurt this bad.

The Blue Bonnet Cafe, from the outside, looked like what Bill's father always called a "greasy spoon joint," but the cleanliness and modern décor on the inside dismissed that notion. Everyone stopped talking and looked at Bill as he walked in. Cathy was sitting in one of the red vinyl covered booths with her back to Bill. She turned and waved him over. He could feel everyone's eyes on him as he crossed the room. When he slid into the booth the voices slowly began to chatter again.

"Sorry, I'm late," Bill said, still trying to catch his breath from his brief jog.

"Did you run here? That wasn't necessary. I have no place else to be. I took the liberty of calling ahead to have the food ready. Hope you don't mind."

Bill started to respond, but a waitress, whose name tag told Bill her name was Sally, placed the biggest chicken fried steak he'd ever seen in front of him. If his brief jog didn't give him a heart attack, he was pretty sure this meal would.

"You timed it just right," Cathy said. "Don't let it get cold."

They began eating in silence at first, but after a few bites Cathy asked, "Did you find anything?"

Bill chewed and swallowed the piece of milk gravy covered meat he had just stuck in my mouth and said, "Nothing yet. I checked everything from that day to about three months after. I checked for stories of dead bodies being recovered, or murders, but apparently you didn't have a lot of crime here. I checked obituaries and discovered that the sheriff at that time died in a car crash about a month after the girl landed on our porch. Then I checked quinceaneras."

"What?"

"You know, the celebrations the Mexicans have when their daughter turns fifteen—"

"I know what a quinceanera is. I just don't know why you were checking them."

"I figured that she was about that age. Thought there might be a picture."

Cathy cocked one eyebrow. "Did you think you would recognize her? After all, I doubt if you saw that much of her face and it's been forty years."

Bill smiled. "I was only six at the time, so her naked body really didn't hold as much fascination as you might think, but when she jumped up and looked at me, I got a good look at that face. I don't think I'll ever forget that face."

"I'm sorry I didn't mean to accuse you of being a perv. I am impressed that you have maintained eye contact with me. Most men keep looking at my boobs." She winked at Bill, and of course Bill immediately glanced down at said boobs.

"They are very nice," he said, "but I'm a reporter first, and man second." He knew it was a lie as soon as he said it, but she didn't call him on it. She did roll her eyes. "Okay, you're right, but boobs don't communicate near as much as the eyes. Cathy, do you know anything about sun tattoos."

She dropped her fork into her plate and gasped.

"What?" Bill asked. "What's wrong?"

"Who have you been talking to?" Cathy asked. She seemed a little angry.

"Just the librarian, but not about tattoos. Why?"

"Why are you asking me, then?"

"The naked Mexican girl had a tattoo of a sun on her shoulder. I didn't remember it, but my mother saw it and told the deputy. I read it in the report."

She took a deep breath and let it out. "Oh, okay. I just thought—"

"Thought what?"

"I thought someone had told you about my tattoo."

Bill chuckled. "Oh, okay. You have a sun tattoo?"

"Yes."

"Is it somewhere you wouldn't mind letting me see it?"

She gave Bill a wry smile. "There's no place I would have a tattoo I wouldn't mind letting you see. I'm quite the exhibitionist, but it's on my thigh. I'll show you, but not here in the diner."

Bill's face went warm. "I'm sorry. I was rude to ask. I was just wondering what it looked like. What I really want to know is where you got it. It might be a lead."

"I got it done in Corpus Christi, but there is a tattoo parlor here in town. It's only been here a few years, though."

"Why did you get it? Does it hold some significance?"

She cut another piece of meat. "I just liked it," she said, and popped the steak into her mouth. Bill, once again, had the feeling that another person was holding back, but he knew people from this area are not too forthcoming with strangers. She might be okay flashing her body, but her thoughts would be kept private.

"Why do you think a young girl would have had such a tattoo back then?" Bill asked.

She shrugged her shoulders and continued chewing. "It was certainly a rare thing back then I imagine" she said, finally.

"Well, let's forget the tattoo. What can you tell me about Forester? It was nearly a ghost town when I lived there. I imagine it is by now."

"That's not entirely accurate. The general store and post office closed, but there is a tourist resort a couple of miles out of town that houses a post office and convenience store. They put a reservoir on the Frio River, so there's a man-made lake there now. Still, there are a few residents that still live in Forester, itself."

"Sounds nice. I should go visit."

Cathy looked down at her plate as her lips curled into a smile. "Maybe you should," she said.

Bill was puzzled by her bemusement but decided to ignore it. "Do you think the old house I lived in would still be there?"

"If it hasn't burned down. It was all wood, wasn't it? We've been in a terrible drought and there have been some bad grass fires out that way. It burned up most of what was left of the town."

"I'd like to go see," Bill said, and then he looked up and saw Sheriff Gutierrez enter the diner.

"Oh shit," he said.

Cathy turned around and looked. "Ricky," she said. "Over here."

"Why did you do that?"

"I want you two to clear things up. Ricky can probably help you if you'll let him."

31

The sheriff sat down next to Cathy and put his arm on the back of booth seat behind her head—a move Bill thought showed, if not affection, then certainly comfortable familiarity. "Mr. Clark, Cathy has chastised me for being rude to you. She would like me to cooperate with you."

"How did she motivate you to do that?" Bill asked.

"Blackmail," Cathy said. "I've known Ricky all his life. I know things about him that I'm sure he doesn't want published in any paper. In fact, he's been known to collapse naked in a few places he shouldn't have."

"I'm sorry, Sheriff," Bill said. "I didn't mean to put you in such a precarious situation."

"I've been in worse situations," the sheriff said, with no trace of a smile. "At any rate, if there is anything I can do to help, please let me know. I have one piece of information that might be of help to you. I have located the deputy that took your mother's statement. He's retired, but he's still alive. He lives in Kerrville."

He handed Bill a piece of paper with the name and address, and then said, "You should be careful chasing ghosts from the past, Mr. Clark."

"You're the second person to give me that warning, Sheriff," Bill said. "You don't really believe in ghosts, do you?"

"I was speaking about ghosts metaphorically. There are a lot of things that have happened in this area through the years. A lot of people have died in mysterious circumstances. You may be stirring up a hornet's nest."

"Thanks for the warning," Bill said. "But I'm pretty determined to get to the bottom of this. I'll drive over to Kerrville tomorrow. I'm thinking of going to Forester this afternoon."

The sheriff frowned. "I wouldn't recommend it. I've had rumors of illegal drug activity in the area—and I mean cartel level activity."

That certainly gave Bill pause. Drug cartels were nothing to mess with, but he didn't think drug cartel members would bother him. "Well, it's going to be important for me to take some pictures for the story."

Ricky sighed. "I'm actually headed out that way, so I'll drive you, if you don't mind. I have to go check out a theft of some farm equipment outside of there."

Bill didn't really like the idea, but the cartel talk had him a little spooked. "Could you join us, Cathy?" Bill asked. His desire to have Cathy along, besides her being easy on the eyes, was because of his paranoia. He didn't know who he could trust, but he was rather certain he couldn't trust the sheriff.

"How about it, Ricky?" Cathy asked.

"The more the merrier," Ricky said, but no merriment showed on his face. "Let me go call my wife, and then we'll go."

CHAPTER 7

The big advantage of going to Forester with the sheriff was the speed in which they got there. Bill sat in the back, behind Ricky, so he couldn't see the speedometer, but the mesquite trees went by as a blur. They had left the Blue Bonnet and less than thirty minutes later we were standing on the porch of Bill's old house. It had not burned down, but it had been long vacated and looked to be about to collapse from neglect.

"Look familiar?" Cathy asked.

Bill snapped several pictures of the front of the house. "It's smaller than I remember."

"Where did the girl fall?" Ricky asked.

Bill pointed to the spot, and then snapped a few shots of it. "Right here, just below this window. I was sitting on the couch inside. Mom thought the girl had tried to knock but passed out before she could."

"Makes sense," Ricky said. "And she was completely naked?"

"As the day she was born."

Ricky stepped to the edge of the porch and looked out. "This was the front porch?" he asked.

"Technically," Bill said, "but everyone who came to visit would come to our back door. The street out front was grown over with brush; just as it is now."

"So, she came out of the woods?" Cathy asked.

Bill nodded and took some pictures of the woods. "She was lucky not to have been bitten by a snake," he said. "Those woods were full of rattlesnakes back then. I imagine they are still. She took off running in that direction. The fence used to be there, but it's gone now."

The sheriff was leaning against one of the porch beams when they heard what sounded like the pop of a rifle. Wood splintered just above Ricky's head. He pulled his gun and shouted, "Get down!"

His warning was unnecessary because Cathy and Bill were both already prone. Ricky was scanning the woods for the would-be assassin.

Bill was lying as low and flat as he could get, but he held up his camera and tried to take some pictures in the direction of where he thought the shot came from. "Why would someone be shooting at us?" he asked.

"They probably aren't," Ricky said. "That sounded like a .22. It's probably just some kids hunting. They have no reason to think anyone else is around. For all we know the bullet ricocheted off a rock."

Cathy asked, "If it's kids, how did they get here? No kids live around here, and I didn't see any cars around."

"I imagine the kids here walk all over these woods," Ricky said. "They are a lot tougher than the Faytonville kids."

About that time, they heard the pop again, this time shattering the glass in the window above Bill. "I don't think these shots are accidental," Bill said.

"I believe you are right," Ricky said. He fired three rounds from his Glock in the general direction of where the shots might be coming from, and then everything was silent.

"How long should we stay here?" Cathy asked. "We're

sitting ducks!"

"I'm going to fire three more rounds, then you two need to run back to the car," Ricky said. "I'll be right behind you. Ready. Go."

Bill and Cathy took off running, trying to keep their heads down. They heard Ricky's shots, but none were returned. Cathy reached the car first, and she opened the back door and dove in. Bill went in after her. Both were crouched in the back seat floorboard. Ricky climbed into the driver's seat and started the car. He threw the car in gear and fishtailed away from the house slinging dirt and gravel. They listened for shots but heard none.

Ricky picked up the radio mike and called for assistance. The dispatcher told him help was on the way. "State troopers will be here soon," he said over the seat. "It's probably safe for you guys to come on up now."

"Do you think you shot them?" Bill asked, as he climbed up into the seat.

"I hope not. I wasn't trying to. I was aiming up high. Still, you never know."

"What do you think that was all about?" Cathy asked.

"I don't know," Ricky said. "It could be a number of things. As I said before, I have received reports that there are some drug activities going on around here. Still, I guess it could be related to the fact that someone may not want a reporter looking into our local ghost."

"How many people know I'm doing a story?" Bill asked. "I just told you two, Chuck, and Charlotte."

Ricky chuckled and said, "By now Chuck and Charlotte have told everyone in town. Chuck has probably even informed everyone in the county."

"You don't really believe someone would try to shoot

Bill because of that, do you, Ricky?" Cathy asked.

Ricky shook his head. "No, I don't. I think that girl that fell on the porch grew up, had lots of babies, and is cooking tortillas for her grandbabies somewhere. And I think Bill here is wasting his time. It was a long time ago."

"I'm not disagreeing with you," Bill said, "but if the shooters were trying to hide a drug operation, wouldn't it be stupid to try and kill a cop with a twenty-two?"

Ricky nodded. "That's a good point. I can't imagine if someone was serious, they'd use a gun that is really only good for shooting rabbits."

"But that raises another point," Bill said. "Why didn't they hit one of us? We're considerably larger targets that rabbits."

Ricky thought about that for a minute. "That's true. He — or she may have missed on purpose."

Bill looked at the pictures he took on the small digital read-out on his camera. He couldn't see anyone, but in one picture there appeared to be what could have been a gun barrel. The shooter seemed to have been close. "I'm a terrible shot, but I think I could've hit one of us with a twenty-two rifle. Maybe they were just trying to scare us or send a message," Bill said.

Bill handed the camera to Ricky, and Ricky studied the picture while still speeding down the highway. He handed the camera back to Bill. "It was definitely a rifle. You're right. If they wanted to hit us, they should have been able to. I need to get back to help the troopers find them. I'm going to have to drop you two off at Fifth Sun. You can wait in the store."

"What's Fifth Sun?" Bill asked.

Cathy smiled. "It's the tourist resort I told you about."

As they pulled up to the resort, Bill noticed that the store looked more like the gatehouse of a high security prison.

On the north side there was a double gate sally port and a high fence with razor wire around the top surrounding the place. "What kind of tourist resort is this?" Bill asked.

"It's a clothing optional resort," Cathy said.

"You mean a nudist colony?" Bill asked.

"They hadn't been called nudist colonies since the sixties. They prefer to call it a resort, but yeah that's basically what it is?" Ricky said.

"We're not going to have to get naked, are we?" Bill asked.

Cathy laughed. "The actual resort is another couple of miles from this gate. This is just a store and post office used by the local ranchers, as well as the tourists. You must pay to go to the resort. You'll not see any naked people and you won't have to get naked."

"Why such tight security?" Bill asked. "I thought nudists liked being seen naked."

"Not by voyeurs, and the neighbors have never really enjoyed having them around," Ricky said. "Most of the ranchers are pretty conservative. They aren't really happy about having this place here. In fact, most of them deny its existence if you ask them about it. As you'll see there will be nothing to indicate that Fifth Sun is a nudist resort. The guests only know about it by actively seeking it on the Internet. The only way to gain entrance is to buy a ticket online. That keeps them from accidentally letting in someone who doesn't know what's what."

"Are other nudist resorts this tight on security?" Bill asked.

"I don't think so," Cathy said, "but I haven't been to any others."

"You've been here?" Bill asked with a slight gasp.

She smirked. "Yes. I'm a reporter. I came to do a story.

They were cooperative, and I wrote a story, but I never printed it. It wouldn't go over well here. My readers don't want to read about naked people. It would have just caused a scandal. I've tried sending it to freelance markets, but no one is interested."

"Did you get naked?"

She winked at Bill. "Of course. I told you I was an exhibitionist. Besides, I had to agree to it before they'd let me come out there."

Bill had no problem with public nudity in theory, but he wondered if he would do it for a story. He thought it might compromise his objectivity. Suddenly it occurred to Bill that this might be connected to his story. "Was this place here when I lived here?" Bill asked.

She raised her eyebrows, and took a long pause, but finally said, "You know, I don't know. It's possible, I imagine. I discovered it on the Internet, but I have no idea how long it has been in existence. Do you, Ricky?"

Ricky shook his head and said nothing.

"I was just thinking that there might be a connection," Bill said. "A naked girl with a sun tattoo collapses on the steps of a house not that far from a nudist resort named Fifth Sun. Seems like more than a coincidence."

"It would be a good thing to research, but you won't be able to get any information from the people in the store." Cathy said. "You'll have to buy a ticket online and go to the resort and get naked to get anything. The guy to talk to is Jeremy Porter."

Bill would have to get Valerie's approval. He didn't think she was going to let him spend that kind of money to go to a nudist resort without a damn good reason. It had been a long time since he and Valerie were smoking pot naked with their friends out at the hot springs. She might not be so opened-minded about it these days, especially with Bill being so far away from home.

CHAPTER 8

The store reminded Bill a lot of the old Forester general store and post office from when he was a kid. It was obvious that they had tried to duplicate it. The wood floor was linoleum designed to look like wood, and the wood stove surrounded by rocking chairs was purely decorative, as there was obviously central air and heat. They even had a replica of the Coke machine with the heavy crank that dispensed six-ounce bottles for a dime back then. Bill would have thought it was the real thing had it not been for the LED display above the coin slot saying a Coke cost a buck fifty.

It had a real nostalgia feel except for the fluorescent lights and the skin-headed, tattooed kid behind the counter. Bill asked him why this place was called Fifth Sun and the kid said, "How the hell should I know? I just work here."

Cathy laughed. "I told you so. Let's go have a seat."

They both took a seat in the rocking chairs by the fake wood stove. "Do you know why the place is called Fifth Sun?" Bill asked Cathy.

"It has to do with the Aztecs. They are known as the 'people of the sun.' They believed that there were different periods of existence of the gods. The periods were referred to as 'suns.' The Aztecs believed there had been five suns, so the last of the Aztecs lived in the period of the fifth sun."

"What has any of that have to do with a nudist resort?"

"Well, nudists are often referred to as sun worshipers."

Bill nodded. "Okay. I see. That does make some sense."

They sat in silence for a moment, and then Cathy asked. "How long have you been married, Bill?"

"Nineteen years."

"To the same woman?"

"Yes, but it's my second marriage. I was married to a girl I met in high school. But it didn't work out. It lasted less than a week."

"Ouch," Cathy said.

"I met Valerie when we were in college. She worked for the school paper and she came to do a story on the place where I was working. I was doing public relations for a law firm that turned out to be a tough job, since three of the four partners were crooks. Valerie's reporting basically put me out of a job. We started dating a few days after they hauled most of the people in the firm out in handcuffs. She took me out to dinner, feeling sorry for me, and we ended up in bed. Next thing we know, we were married, and I used my savings to buy the paper."

"So, you've only been with the two women?"

"By 'been with,' do you mean sex?"

Cathy laughed. "Yeah, I guess so."

"There have been a few others."

"Have you ever cheated on Valerie?"

Bill turned and looked at her. "Am I talking to you, or the press?" he asked

"I'll agree to keep it off the record, and keep it out of the press, but I can't promise anything about the gossip chain. That's a small-town loyalty I can't ignore," she said, with a laugh.

"Okay, I guess I can live with that. No, I've never cheated on my wife, but part of the reason is that I'm constantly accusing her of cheating. Part of the reason why I'm here is to work through my trust issues"

She looked at Bill with a confused expression

"My mother left my dad soon after the girl on the porch event. She supposedly ran off with another man, and I never saw her again. My father told me she had died, but my therapist thinks my father might have lied about that. At any rate, I'm here is to find out what happened to my mother."

"Wow, that's pretty heavy," Cathy said. "So, there's a possibility that you might even find your mother."

Bill shrugged and said, "I suppose, but that seems unlikely after all these years. Besides, I think my mother would have found me if she'd wanted to. Even if she is alive, I doubt if she will want to have anything to do with me."

"Well, I agree with your therapist. You need to know. It's bound to change your thought processes."

"It was my wife that pushed me to do this, but I really don't want to talk about this anymore. What about you? What's your story?"

"Off the record?" she asked.

"Yes, but I want the same gossip rights."

She laughed. "Fair enough. I cheated on my husband with Ricky."

Bill nodded and said, "I thought you and Ricky seemed a little chummy."

"Well, Ricky went back to his wife, but it was over for Jerry and me long before I cheated with Ricky. The Gazette belonged to him. I was stunned that he let me buy him out. He's still pretty pissed, but he went easy on me."

"I'm sorry. That must be tough. Are you dating anyone now?"

She smiled sadly and said, "Nope, I'm completely man-free at the moment."

"Is that the way you prefer it?"

"Well, that's what I keep telling myself, anyway. I don't want any of the men I have had, but I am always looking for someone new. Not a lot of potential in Faytonville. The only eligible bachelor these days is Chuck Tremaine, and you've probably guessed that I'm not his type."

Bill laughed. "I think you're right about that."

"Would you care for a beer?" Cathy said, standing and walking over to one of the coolers behind them.

Bill pointed to the sign that said that it was illegal to consume alcohol on these premises.

"Unless you're working for Texas Alcohol and Beverage Commission," she said. "No one else is going to care."

She pulled out a six-pack of Coronas. The kid behind the counter looked up and nodded. He went back to reading his novel. She grabbed a lime out of another cooler. There was a knife and a church key lying on the fake wood stove. Cathy opened a couple of Coronas with the church key and used the knife to cut lime wedges that they squeezed into the long neck bottles. Apparently, this happened all the time.

The beer made the afternoon go faster and Cathy and Bill shared their total life stories, or, at least, Bill told his. They talked about everything from their first bicycles to losing their virginity.

The conversation lulled finally, and Cathy raised her Corona in the air, and said, "Here's to finding your mother."

Bill thought about what Charlotte had said back at the library about looking for ghosts of the past. Reluctantly, Bill raised his beer bottle, too.

CHAPTER 9

By the time Ricky returned to pick Bill and Cathy up they'd finished one six pack and started on another. Ricky seemed a little pissed that they were rather intoxicated.

"You guys will be lousy company on the trip back," he said.

"Did you find anything?" Bill asked.

"Nothing. Not even the shell casings."

"Sounds like a pro," Cathy said.

Ricky scowled. "You watch too many cop shows. Picking up their brass doesn't necessarily mean it was a pro. My mother always taught me to pick up my casings for environmental reasons. Some people do their own reloading, but twenty-two shells are relatively cheap, so I doubt that is why they picked up their casings."

"I thought we'd already established that it wasn't a pro," Bill said. "Pros wouldn't use a twenty-two."

"That's not entirely true," Ricky replied. "At close range, they can be rather precise, especially with a silencer. Still, I don't think it was a pro. Can you guys make it to the car? Or do I need to borrow the store's hand truck?"

Cathy and Bill laughed and struggled to their feet. In the car Cathy was fast asleep in the passenger's side minutes after they hit the road.

"So, I imagine with Cathy drinking all that 'truth serum' that she filled you in on everything about us?" Ricky asked, when he thought she was knocked out.

"A little," Bill said glancing up at him in the rear-view mirror "She didn't really go into a lot of detail."

"She's a great lady," he said, "but a little dangerous. You better watch yourself."

"I'm married."

He chuckled. "Yeah, so was I."

Ricky dropped Bill off at the Motel Six where he had made a reservation. Ricky told Bill that his car would be fine at the courthouse, and that it was only six blocks away. "I'll give you a ride in the morning, if you want me to," he said.

"Nah, I will need the fresh air. Tell Cathy I had a good time." Cathy didn't stir. Bill wondered if Ricky was going to have to carry her into her house. Oh well, it wasn't any of his business.

Bill checked into his room and took a shower. He hadn't been that drunk to begin with, but he was already feeling sober. It was only about six in the evening, and Bill was a little hungry, but he didn't want to walk all the way to the Blue Bonnet. He noticed there was a Dairy Queen across the street. That would work.

To Bill's surprise the restaurant was nearly empty. There was only one other customer. Coincidentally, it was one of the few people in town Bill had already met. Sitting in a booth in the far west corner was Chuck Tremaine. Bill ordered his food, and they gave him a big piece of plastic with a number on it. Bill didn't know why the girl behind the counter felt Bill needed a number. Bill took his number and headed towards Chuck's table. He sat down in front of him and said, "Hello, Mr. Tremaine, mind if I join you? I hate eating alone."

"Yes, I do mind. I prefer eating alone. That is why I come out here to this stupid fast-food place instead of the Blue Bonnet."

"You take your reputation as the biggest sorehead in town pretty seriously, don't you?"

"My reputation is that I'm the biggest asshole in town, and it isn't true. There is a lot of competition if you ask me."

"Okay, I am asking you. Who would you say the other assholes are?"

He snorted. "It would be easier to list the people that are not."

"I've only met a few: the sheriff, newspaper editor, and librarian."

"Out those three, only Charlotte Brown would make the 'non-asshole' list."

As County Clerk, Ricky would be one of his superiors, so certainly he would dislike Ricky, but why Cathy? I had no doubt that Cathy's female charms were wasted on him, but what had she done to upset him?

"So, you like Charlotte?" Bill asked.

"I didn't say that. I just said she isn't an asshole. She is bright, articulate, and honest. I respect her, but that doesn't mean I like her. I generally hate other people."

"Generally? So, there are other people you actually like?"

"I've grown some affection for the people I have known in the past. Most of them are dead--my parents, for example. I had a good friend, Frankie, who died last year. Other than that, I don't care for people. Especially people who insist on butting into other people's lives when they've been politely told to bug off."

"I don't agree with the 'politely' part, but I'll go," Bill said, getting to his feet. "First, let me just ask you a couple questions. How long have you been the county clerk?"

"Thirty-two years."

"Wow, you must be getting close to retirement."

Chuck snorted, again. Bill imagined that snort of his was the closest he ever came to actually laughing. "No county employee ever retires. I'll die with my head smacking against my computer keyboard someday. It will probably take them a week to find me."

"That sounds sad."

He sneered. "Spare me your sympathy."

"Okay, Chuck. Just let me ask my second question. In your thirty-two years, who all has been down in the basement you took me into this morning?"

The waitress brought out Chuck's food on a tray and handed it to him and took away his plastic number.

"No one goes down there besides the slut at the newspaper. Today was the first time I've seen the sheriff go down there." He picked up his burger. "Now if you don't mind. I'd like to eat my burger in peace."

The waitress brought out Bill's food as he walked away from Chuck's table. "Could you put that in a bag for me?" Bill asked. "I think I'll just take it with me."

As he walked outside, Bill couldn't help but notice the pick-up in the parking lot. It was a four-wheel drive Ford with a heavy-duty grill guard on the front. The large tires were caked with mud. It could not have belonged to anyone but Chuck, but it certainly didn't look like the kind of vehicle Chuck would drive. It looked like the kind of truck that might have had a rifle rack back before the school shootings and gun control.

He wondered if Chuck had a rifle. Maybe even a twenty-two caliber. That would seem ludicrous, but one never knows. Chuck was glaring at Bill through the restaurant's window, so Bill didn't attempt to sneak a peek.

Bill went back to his room and ate his chicken strips

while watching television. After he finished eating, he called home.

"How'd it go today?" Valerie asked.

"Well, I got shot at."

"What?"

"Someone shot at us while we were at the old homestead."

"Who is 'we?'"

"The sheriff, the newspaper lady, and me."

"By 'newspaper lady' you mean the blonde and beautiful Cathy. You two seem to be getting pretty chummy."

"Valerie, you know she's the logical person to be helping me. There's no need to be all suspicious and jealous."

Valerie laughed. "You're such a hypocrite. Still, I agree that she's probably a good resource. Just don't let her help too much. Do you think your inquiries have drawn someone's attention?"

"I'm not sure. The sheriff thinks it could've been some druggies, but he didn't seem too convinced."

Bill heard her scratching notes on a notepad. Once a reporter, always a reporter.

"While you're taking notes. Could you look something up on the Internet for me?"

"Sure. What do you want me to look up?"

"Fifth Sun. It's a nudist resort outside of Forester."

There was a long silence on the other end of the phone, but then Bill could hear the computer keys clicking. "Looks like a nice place," she said, finally. "Why are you asking?"

"There might be a connection between that place and the girl."

"Are you going out there?"

"Actually, I've already been out there. I got as close to it as I could today without getting naked."

"Are you planning on getting naked?" she asked.

"I was just curious how much it cost to be a guest there. I thought I'd try to go out there undercover, so to speak. Which would mean, yes, I would have to get naked."

Again, there was a long silence and then the clicking of the keys. "It's twenty dollars for a day pass, but forty if you are a single male." she said. "It's a hundred if you want to stay the night, but again it's two hundred if you are a single male."

"That's not so bad. I'm sure I could get what I need with a day pass."

"You have to get a pass online. You want me to get one for you?"

"Not yet. I don't think I have enough information to go out there right now."

She laughed. "Are you a little nervous about public nudity? You've been naked in public before, but that was pre 'love handle' days."

"The crowds were much smaller at the hot springs. I was much younger and leaner, but I won't know any of these people, and will never see them again."

"Do what you got to do, Bill."

Bill realized that this was one of the reasons he loved this woman. She trusted him. He just wished he could feel the same way. He didn't think he would have ever been able to tell Valerie to do the same. He felt his anger rising at the thought of her stripping down at some resort almost a thousand miles away. "I've got a couple of other leads for now. I'll save getting naked for last. Probably won't even happen."

"If you feel you need to, go ahead," Valerie said. "But

don't get any ideas of taking up that lifestyle. My nudist days are over." She paused, and then asked, "If you go, will you take Cathy with you?"

Bill hadn't thought of that. She'd been there before. She probably wouldn't mind, but Bill considered Ricky's warning. "It would be cheaper, but probably not," Bill said. "I think that would blow my cover."

"Whatever," she said, a little too casually. Bill knew Valerie was not quite as secure as she pretended to be.

"I'm sure her boobs hang down to her knees when she's naked," Bill said.

"You're so full of shit."

Bill laughed. "Guilty as charged. I guess I'll let you go. I plan to head for Kerrville in the morning."

"Be careful, Bill. I love you."

"Love you, too. Goodnight."

CHAPTER 10

Kerrville was a little less than a hundred miles away as the crow flies, but there was no straight route from Faytonville. Bill had planned to go by himself, but Cathy met him by his car and asked to go with him. Cathy saved Bill from having to try and decipher the GPS instructions. She even knew where the retired deputy's house was.

Faron Cole was about seventy, which put him in his early twenties when he took Bill's mother's statement. Bill had called ahead and made an appointment to see him. He was sitting on his front porch waiting for them when they pulled up. He stood and he smiled broadly when he saw Cathy. "Well, I'll be. Cathy Dale, what in the Sam hill are you doing here?"

She embraced him and said, "Hi, Uncle Faron. I thought it was about time to come see you and since this man was coming anyway, I decided to tag along."

"Uncle?" Bill asked.

"He and my father were hunting buddies, among other things," Cathy explained. "He's not my blood relative, but just as good as."

It was not a big surprise to Bill that she knew the man. People in small towns all know each other. That was to be expected. However, this relationship seemed rather close and it seemed to Bill that she should have offered him that information.

Cathy introduced Bill and the man offered his hand. The old man took it with a grip firmer than necessary. "Can I get you something to drink?" the old man asked. Back in Copper

City, if someone offered Bill a drink it usually meant a beer or other spirits. Here in Texas, he probably meant sweet iced tea. "Sure, I'll take some iced tea," Bill said, proud of himself for not making a social faux pas.

"I'm sorry, son, but I'm a Latter-day Saint. I've got some lemonade, though."

So much for pride, but Bill assured himself there was no way for him to know the man was a Mormon. "That would be great," Bill said.

Mr. Cole was not a big man. He stood only a few inches above Cathy. He was rail thin and seemed to be in really good shape. He told them how his wife had died a couple of years back and how he thought that the funeral was the last time he'd seen Cathy. He and Cathy reminisced for a while and Bill let them. Eventually the old man got around to asking Bill about his religious beliefs, which Bill had guessed he would. Latter-day Saints were among the largest proselytes in the country, next to Baptists and Jehovah's Witnesses.

"I was raised Southern Baptist," Bill said, "but I don't really practice religion much these days."

"Well, I know you didn't come to be preached to, but I'd sure like to tell you about a better way. The prophet can help you find happiness."

"I've no doubt, Mr. Cole," Bill said, "but I'm not really here on my own time. I'm on company time. Otherwise, I'd be glad to talk religion with you."

"I can certainly respect that. Then we better get to it."

Bill pulled his notebook out of his pocket. "I want to talk to you about a report my mother gave you about forty years ago about a naked Mexican girl passing out on our front porch."

His thick gray eyebrows shot up. "Land sakes alive, Son. I hadn't thought about that in years. Betty Jean Clark was your mama?"

"Yes sir. I just wanted to find out what that was all about. There didn't seem to be much of an investigation. All I found was your report, and nothing else."

The old man's face darkened. "Well, you might not have found any other reports, but Sheriff Prine did an investigation. He interviewed everyone in the county. If he hadn't died, I'm sure he would've found that girl. I know he did find a name."

"Really? There wasn't a name in your report."

"Because, like I said, he found the name, not me. After I turned in my initial report, the sheriff took over. It was a big deal to him. You need to find his report. I'm not sure where it would be. He never filed anything officially, but I'm sure there are some notes somewhere."

"Do you remember the girl's name?"

"The last name was Rosales, but I can't remember her first name."

"And you guys never found her?"

"Like I said, it was only a big deal to the sheriff. When the sheriff died, the interest died with him. All that survived were the ghost stories."

I knew my next question was going to sound crazy, but it begged to be asked. "Do you think the sheriff's death was an accident?"

Mr. Cole frowned. "According to the accident report, Sheriff Prine's car went off the road at eighty miles an hour and hit a tree. The car burst into flames. It was speculated that he had a heart attack while he was driving."

"And do you believe that is what happened?" Bill asked.

"I believe that the report was accurate."

"Why is that?"

"Because of who wrote it?"

"And who was that?"

"My father," Cathy said.

CHAPTER 11

Bill realized that if he had been a really good reporter, he would have already known that the person he'd spent the better part of two days with was actually a lead. Still, why hadn't she told him she knew this deputy and that her father was also a deputy? Did she not feel it was necessary? Or was there a trust issue involved? She might have saved Bill a lot of trouble.

"Well," Bill said, "I think I will have some questions for Cathy on the ride home, but I don't think I need anything else from you, Mr. Cole--wait, there is one other thing. What do you know about the Fifth Sun nudist resort?"

He laughed. "Well, I can tell you I ain't never been there. That's for darn sure."

"What about when you were a deputy? Nothing ever happened out there?"

"Not after it became a nudie place. Before that, yeah, we went out there."

"Really?" Bill asked. "What was it before?"

He shrugged. "We called it a church encampment back then, but they would probably call it a compound these days."

"Are you saying it was a cult?"

The old man smiled. "That word gets thrown around a lot these days, but it didn't back then. My church has been called a cult, and we've been given a pretty hard time since what occurred over at Eldorado."

"You're talking about the polygamists?" Bill asked.

He winced. "Right. They're a totally different bunch from us, but people don't separate us from them in their minds."

"What did these people at Fifth Sun believe?"

"I have no idea. As far as I could tell, they minded their own business and stayed clear of the rest of us. Every so often a local rancher would accuse them of stealing sheep. We'd go out there and look around, but we never found any evidence. They were all pleasant and friendly and welcomed us with open arms when we went out there."

"You never had a complaint of kidnapping or anything more sinister?"

The man thought for a minute, then looked at Cathy. "No, not about those people. We had a few runaways and missing persons, but none of them connected to Fifth Sun."

Cathy nodded in agreement.

"So, the encampment was also called Fifth Sun back then?" I asked.

"Yes. Yes, it was."

"Was it mostly Mexican people in the church?"

"It was in the beginning, but the fellow that became their leader was an Anglo and by the late seventies it was almost all Anglos. Then around '82, it turned into that nudist colony."

"Do you know that man's name?"

"He called himself Jeremiah Ray, but I doubt if that was his real name."

"Could his real name have been Porter?" Bill asked.

The old man shrugged.

"Well, I guess that's all I need," Bill said and closed his notebook.

Twenty minutes out of Kerrville Bill turned to Cathy. "Why didn't you tell me about your father?" Bill asked.

"You didn't ask?"

"But didn't you think it was relevant to what I was doing?"

"Why?" she asked, quite sincerely. As if she really didn't see the connection.

"Well, first of all, was he a deputy at the time that girl collapsed on our porch?"

"Yes. Yes, he was."

Bill frowned. "So, is it possible that you know more about the story than you previously told me?"

"I was born just before that incident, so why would I know any more about something that happened back then? I was just a kid. A baby, actually."

Putting Cathy on the defensive was the last thing Bill wanted to do, but he could tell she was playing it close to the vest. She knew more about what was going on than she was willing to tell him.

"Chuck Tremaine says that you are the only person who goes down to the basement where the records are kept. You're a reporter, so that makes sense. It also makes sense that you've investigated this story and know more about it than you are willing to share. Maybe you already know that there isn't a story, or maybe there is, and you don't want me to scoop you."

"There may be a story," she said, "but I wouldn't expect a Pulitzer for it. I don't give a rat's ass about your naked girl. The only story I've ever worked on has to do with the death of Sheriff Prine. My father was never really sure that he died by accident."

"But your father did the report."

She bit her bottom lip. She seemed to be considering whether she should talk to Bill about this.

"What are you worried about?" Bill asked.

"My father is dead. He died three years ago of an apparent suicide. Only I don't think it was suicide and I think it's connected to the death of Sheriff Prine. Yes, the report my father did was accurate, but he never believed the conclusion."

"I don't understand."

"The heart attack was purely conjecture on the coroner's part, but everyone knew Sheriff Prine was healthy as a horse. And he never got his car over sixty miles an hour."

"Not even in a chase."

"There were no chases. Back then if he flashed his lights people pulled over."

Bill decided that she was leveling with him. "So where are you on the story now?" Bill asked.

"I've all but given up," she said. "I'm no detective, and the trail is too cold to follow. My father had tried for years, and he couldn't find anything. So, what chance did I have? Ricky has tried to help me, but he's not been able to do much either."

"Do you think--" Bill started to ask, but there was a loud bang and the car swerved out of control. Bill fought the steering wheel and just about had it under control when the front wheel hit the soft shoulder and they barreled into large irrigation ditch. Water flooded over the windshield, and then started pouring in around the passenger side door. Cathy's jeans were getting soaked.

"Are you okay?" Bill asked.

Her eyes were wide, but she nodded. She undid her seatbelt and grabbed Bill's arm and pulled trying to get out of the muddy water. Bill opened his door and awkwardly pulled her up over him and out of the car. Once she was out, he undid his belt and climbed out behind her.

"What the hell happened?" Cathy asked.

Bill looked at the car and saw that all four tires were

blown out. "Something punctured all our tires." Bill walked up the road, back the way they had come. Cathy followed. They reached the spot where they had blown the tires and saw the device that had caused the problem.

"What is that?" Cathy asked.

"It's a spike strip. It's what police use to stop high speed chases."

"What's it doing here?"

Bill looked around and saw no one. "I don't know, but I don't think this was left out by neglect. I'm afraid it might be more than a coincidence that we've been nearly killed twice in two days."

Cathy looked around and began to shiver. It might've been from her wet pants, but Bill thought it had more to do with what he had just said. The same chill went through him, knowing that they were standing out in the wide open. "Maybe we should find some cover," Bill said.

There was a small stand of trees to the right of them, and they headed for it. Bill pulled out his cell phone and dialed the emergency number. He explained his situation and the dispatcher promised that help was on the way.

Bill and Cathy crouched between two trees. "Do you really think someone did this intentionally to us?" Cathy asked. There was a quiver in her voice.

"Well, it might not be, but it does seem odd," Bill said. "Did you tell anyone we were coming up here?"

She shook her head. "I know what you're thinking. Ricky didn't do this."

"I didn't say he did, but who else with access to this kind of equipment would?"

"I don't know."

"Look, Cathy," Bill said with frustration, "Whether it

is about the girl, or the death of the sheriff, I think we've got someone's attention. The person, or persons, involved is trying to send us a message."

"That car accident could've killed us!" Cathy exclaimed.

Bill nodded. "If I'd been driving faster, it probably would have."

"This is getting more serious."

"It would seem so."

A state trooper arrived first. He was stunned to see the device that blew out the tires. "I don't know who it belongs to, but it's not any local law enforcement," he said. "Law enforcement equipment is usually easy to trace. Still, this was probably stolen. Ya'll can leave your phone numbers with me and I'll let you know if I find anything, but I don't think I will."

The wrecker arrived and pulled the car out of the ditch. The driver took them back to Kerrville. The mechanic told them at the garage that the car wouldn't be ready until the next day, if that.

"It's a rental," Bill said. "I'll probably be able to get a replacement."

"Yeah," The mechanic said, "but it'll still probably be tomorrow before you can get one. Everything's shut down for the folk festival."

He gave them a ride to a motel called the Swiss Clock Inn. Bill stared at the office of the motel, but he didn't go in right away.

"What is the problem?" Cathy asked.

"I'm trying to figure out how I'm going to explain two motel room bills to my wife."

"I don't mind sharing a room," she said.

"That would be even harder to explain."

"Then don't tell her. But make up your mind. I want to get out of these wet pants."

"What are you going to wear?" Bill asked.

She laughed. "What do you expect me to wear? I'll wrap a towel around myself."

As it turned out, one room was all that was available, because of the folk festival. The room did have two beds. "It's okay, Bill," Cathy said. "We're both adults. Nothing will happen that we don't want to happen."

Bill nodded, but he didn't find her comment reassuring.

They got inside the room and Cathy didn't bother waiting until she got to the bathroom to shuck her jeans. Bill attempted to avert his eyes, but there was a mirror on the wall he turned to and he could still see her.

Bill said, "I'm going to go get us some food."

Cathy pulled off her blouse exposing her bra that matched her panties. "I'm going to get a shower. Pick me up a burger with fries and a Diet Coke."

Bill walked out just as she was unhooking her bra. This was going to be a long night.

Bill didn't know why he hadn't noticed the man standing by the coke machine. At first, he thought the man was staring at him, but at second glance the man seemed to be counting out change. He was a short Mexican man wearing a straw cowboy hat that had been sweated on a lot. As Bill started across the street, he saw the man in his peripheral vision pocket his change and walk away. He might have just changed his mind, but Bill was more than just a little paranoid at this point.

CHAPTER 12

Bill returned with the food and knocked, even though he had the key. Cathy opened the door. She stood there with a towel wrapped around her head and another wrapped around her torso. Her matching bra and panties were hanging from the hangers in the closet, along with her t-shirt and jeans.

"Great!" she said. "I'm starved." She took the bag from Bill's hands, removed her food items, and handed Bill back the bag. She plopped down on the bed and began devouring her food. Bill took his food to the desk and sat with his back to her. He pulled open the curtain and looked out the window for the Mexican man, but he didn't see him.

"Relax, Bill," Cathy said. "I won't rape you."

Bill turned to face her. He decided not to tell her about the man. "I'm sure," Bill said, "but it's still a little hard to relax under the circumstances."

She laughed. "Yeah, I imagine you haven't shared too many hotel rooms with a nearly naked lady you barely know."

"It seemed to happen all the time in the sixties spy movies, and it certainly was one of my fantasies, but it's a little different than I imagined."

She pulled the towel off her head and began rubbing her hair with it. "Fantasy is always better than reality," she said.

She stood up and the other towel fell to the floor. She made a slow attempt to retrieve it. Bill turned away. "Sorry," she said. "The towel has been retrieved and back in place."

"No apology necessary. You're very beautiful."

She chuckled. "Thanks. A lady always likes to hear that when she accidently flashes someone."

"This seems like a convenient time to ask," Bill said. "Would you mind if I took a picture of your tattoo?"

She smiled. "I'm impressed, Bill. You're a real professional. Here you have a naked lady and a camera, and all you want is a picture of the tattoo."

"It's all for research," Bill said.

He took the pictures, and then Cathy crawled under the covers of the bed. A few moments later Cathy was snoring. Bill couldn't sleep, but he didn't call Valerie, either. He was sure she would instinctively know Cathy was in the room with him. He would tell her later what happened, and hoped she would understand, even though he wouldn't if the roles were reversed.

The rental company delivered another car to Bill the next morning just before check-out time. Cathy and Bill ate at a diner in Kerrville, and then drove back to Faytonville. Bill watched the road carefully as they drove and kept a nervous eye in the rearview. Bill was worn out when he pulled up in front of the Gazette office. "I have some bourbon in my desk," Cathy said. "Want to come in for a drink?"

"I think I'll just head for the hotel," Bill said. "I'm pretty tired."

"Okay. Do you know what you're going to do next?"

"I'm not sure. I'm going to have to think about it for a little while. Hopefully, I'll find something that won't lead to another attempt to kill me."

She smiled and nodded. "I'll be at the Blue Bonnet around seven. Join me for supper?"

"Sure," he said. Bill watched her until she was safely inside the office. Bill thought he would have felt better had she just climbed into her car and headed for home. Still, he had the feeling that this lady knew how to take care of herself.

Bill's plans included talking to the priest who had served in Forester at that time. He found his name in the reports about the quinceaneras. He found that he was retired and living there in Faytonville. Priests, and other clergy, are sometimes great sources of information, but after what happened today, he felt he needed a heart to heart with the sheriff first. All of it would wait until he got a good nap. Bill ended up sleeping the rest of the afternoon.

Supper, which is Texas for "dinner," with Cathy turned out to be more productive than Bill expected. "You were looking for the rest of the information on that naked girl's investigation," Cathy said, "but it didn't occur to me that you could probably find Sheriff Prine's notes in his personal effects at the Fayton County Museum."

"Why would his notes be there?"

"He never filed any official reports on anything. He just took a lot of notes and stuffed them in his personal filing cabinets. When he died, they set up a display at the museum with all his furniture, including his filing cabinets."

"Do you think the curator would let me see it?"

Cathy laughed and said, "We really don't have what you would seriously call a curator. Not too many people visit the museum, but there's a bunch of us that have keys, and we take turns opening and closing the place."

"So, you can let me in?" Bill asked. Tommy at the store they give

"Absolutely."

Bill gulped down a swig of coffee and said, "Then what are we waiting for?"

Reporting news for small town papers is mostly flying by the seat of one's pants. There are courses taught and taken, but there are just some things a course can't teach. Bill's plan was to talk to the sheriff and the old priest, but now he had found himself again in the company of lovely Cathy.

Bill hadn't called Valerie, yet. He was afraid she would hear the guilt in his voice, although he'd not really done anything wrong. He just spent the night in a motel room with a beautiful naked blonde.

Cathy related to Bill that the museum was once a hotel with thirty-five rooms. The rooms were filled with different exhibits pertaining to Faytonville's past. There were displays about the history of all the churches, the schools, and even hospitals. The third floor, the floor they were looking for, was dedicated to local law enforcement.

"All of these rooms are set up to look like the offices of the sheriffs that died in the line of duty," Cathy explained. "There was a lot of debate over Sheriff Prine since most people believe that he just died in a stupid car wreck, but he was on duty at the time, so we moved his things here.

"In the oldest exhibit is the office of Sheriff Pete Throckmorton who we claim got shot down in the street in 1872 by the gunslinger Clay Allison."

"Really? Is that true?" Bill asked.

"You've heard of Clay Allison?"

"I'm sort of a fan of the Old West. I've read quite a few books about the gunslingers. I've been to Clay Allison's grave in Pecos. They say he literally died falling off the wagon. He was drunk and a wagon wheel decapitated him."

"Yep, that's him. Actually, there's no historical evidence that Clay Allison had ever been to this part of Texas, but he was one of the few gunslingers that actually could do the quick draw and shoot someone. Witnesses at the time said that's what happened to Throckmorton, so they just gave Allison the credit —or the blame."

Bill nodded. "I'd love to spend some time in that exhibit, but I guess I better get straight to Sheriff Prine's exhibit."

Cathy unlocked the door and opened it. She walked in and flipped on the lights. Bill followed her. The room smelled of stale cigarette smoke. Bill noticed an ashtray on the green metal desk in the middle. It had about ten cigarette butts crushed out in it.

Cathy followed his gaze. "We really go for authenticity here," she said, with a laugh. "Those are actually the butts that were in the ashtray when they moved his stuff over here. Sheriff Prine was a chain smoker."

Bill glanced at the rifles on the rack above the desk. "Are those loaded?"

She shrugged. "Probably."

One of the rifles was a .22 caliber. Not usually a law enforcement weapon, but a small-town sheriff might have call to shoot vermin. Nothing unusual about a .22 in a rifle rack. Still, Bill took it off the rack and sniffed the chamber. He couldn't smell anything, but that really did mean that it hadn't been fired lately.

Along the wall opposite the desk, were five gray five-drawer filing cabinets. There were no labels on them. "Do you have any idea where the file I'd be looking for would be?" Bill asked.

"We put the cabinets in here the same exact way he had them in his office," Cathy said. "My guess is that he started with the top drawer on right and filled the cabinets by year. He was sheriff for twenty-one years, so I'd say the file in question would be in the last cabinet on the right, maybe near the top."

Bill walked over and opened the drawer. It was filled with file folders stuffed with yellow legal pad paper. None of the folders were labeled. Bill pulled out the first file in the drawer. It was filled with notes about a break-in of an abandoned warehouse. There was a date. It was three months before the girl on the porch had happened so Bill went further back. He found a file and written across the file folder in blue ink were the words: "Missing Mexican Girl."

"Bingo," Bill said. "You have good instincts."

"Comes with the territory."

Bill laid the file on the desk and opened it up. There was a blurry black and white picture lying on top. It stunned Bill a little.

"Who's that?" Cathy asked.

"That was my mother?" Bill said in almost a whisper. He hadn't seen her face in forty years, and through those years her face had become fuzzy. His memories came back to him with some clarity now.

"Pretty. She looks familiar."

Bill's heart leapt. "You've seen her?"

"I don't know," she said, "but she looks like someone I've seen. Not sure who. I'll think on it. It'll come to me. Obviously, she is much older now, and people do change."

Bill had the same vague feeling of familiarity, but how many women had he stared at since he'd become aware of the possibility of her being alive? Dozens?

The picture was taken on the front porch of the house in Forester. She was pointing at the spot where the girl had fallen.

"There's a reflection of the photographer in window," Bill said. "Can you tell who it is?"

Cathy leaned down and squinted. "Oh my God! That's my dad."

Besides the picture, there was a huge stack of notes on yellow legal pad paper. The sheriff's handwriting was worse than Bill's, and Bill noticed there wasn't a complete sentence anywhere. There were lines on the paper, but the old sheriff obviously didn't use them as guides.

Bill dragged a chair from the other side of the room and offered it to Cathy. She sat in it as Bill took a seat in the wooden desk chair. The chair was on a swivel, and Bill imagined the sheriff spent a lot of time leaning back with his feet up on the desk, because the springs were completely sprung. Bill sat, rather precariously, on the edge, while dividing the stack of papers.

"You try and decipher this bunch and I'll look at this," Bill said, pulling out his leather Moleskine notebook. Cathy pulled out a notebook of her own. It was exactly like his.

Bill began reading, and from what he could tell, the sheriff had spoken to all the ranchers in the area. Most of them hadn't seen anything. One of the ranchers came up with a possible name: Teresa Rosales, but didn't really know if that was the same girl. The young Teresa had done some cooking for the family when the rancher's wife had been sick.

One lady, just outside of Forester, mentioned that someone had taken one of her sheets off the clothesline. The sheriff had asked her how she knew that someone had taken it, and that it just hadn't blown away. Her reply was, "Sheriff, I've been hanging up clothes for twenty years, and I sure as hell know how to pin a sheet so it won't blow away." Bill smiled. That lady was probably dead by now, but he wrote down her name.

"Here's something interesting," Cathy said. "He made a note to himself to check into any missing people or dead bodies between the years 1947 and 1957?"

"That would have been years before the incident. Did he find anything?" Bill asked.

"No, but there was a body found in the Frio in fifty-nine," Cathy said.

"I still don't see a connection."

She shook her head. "It was a thirty-year-old Mexican man. There was an abdominal wound in the side and the body was severely burned. It was burned post-mortem, though."

"Do you suppose we could find a record of that autopsy? Like I said, I don't see a connection, but apparently the sheriff did."

"The Frio River is two hundred miles long, so no telling where the body was found. I'm sure Sheriff Prine checked it out and decided it wasn't relevant. This man was undocumented. There probably wasn't even an autopsy done. His family back in Mexico probably never knew what happened to him. A fairly common story. Even today."

Bill shook his head. "Well, you never know. Is there anything in what you've looked at about Fifth Sun?"

She leafed through her pages. "I don't see anything," she said. "Fifth Sun would have probably been a ranch back then."

"Did the man have a sun tattoo?" Bill asked.

"Doesn't say, but the body would been too burned to tell probably."

"Well, the sun tattoo may not have anything to do with this. Yours doesn't."

Cathy said nothing. Bill noted her silence but decided not to pursue it. She'd tell him when she was ready. She would certainly know how to dodge questions. "It's still too much of a long shot," he said, finally.

Cathy laughed and said, "In other words, you don't have enough justification to go out there, yet."

"No, not yet."

Suddenly a large red-haired man in a plaid flannel shirt appeared in the doorway. He looked really angry. "Cathy, what the hell?" he said.

Cathy went pale, took a deep breath, and spoke. "Bill, I'd like you to meet my husband Jerry Elkins," she said. "He's the Faytonville mayor and I guess he would be the ipso facto curator of this museum."

CHAPTER 13

"I thought you were divorced," Bill said.

"We are," Cathy said, "but he's the only husband I've had, so I still refer to him as my husband. Old habit."

Bill stood and offered his hand. Jerry didn't take it. "Have you slept with her, yet?" he asked.

Bill didn't dignify the question with an answer. There could never really be a correct answer to a question like that.

"What are you doing here, Jerry?" Cathy asked.

"Don't you think that is what I should ask?"

Cathy sighed and asked, "Do we really have to do this?"

"This is an exhibit, Cathy. You're not supposed to be in here. Put those papers back immediately. Just the way you found them."

"Lighten up, Jerry," Cathy said. "It's not like we have the Magna Carta here."

"Value is not the issue."

"What is the issue?" Bill asked.

Jerry's face turned purple.

"It's okay," Bill said. "I'll put the file back just like I found it. I apologize for any disrespect for your artifacts. We're finished."

Jerry glared at Bill. "I guess you're some big city boy thinking that we're a bunch of hicks, and that the history of our little town doesn't amount to shit."

"Actually, I was born in Cotulla and raised some in Forester, which is why I'm here. I, now, live in a town that's actually a little smaller than Faytonville."

His face didn't soften. If anything, he looked angrier.

"You remember the story of the naked Mexican girl?" Cathy asked.

Jerry's mouth dropped open, and he slowly nodded.

Cathy pointed at Bill. "It was his front porch she collapsed on," she said

"I-uh-thought that was an old wives' tale," Jerry said.

Cathy laughed and said, "Well, now you can hear from someone besides your old wife."

"I was just wanting to know what happened," Bill said. "My wife thought it might make a good human-interest story, so I've come back to check it out. Since there have been two attempts on my life, I'm beginning to think more is involved."

Jerry sneered. "You're imagining things, I'm sure. But you probably shouldn't be trying to dig up ghosts from the past."

"No," Bill said. "I'm not imagining things. I've been shot at and someone blew out all the tires on my rental car. I also think it's odd that people keep warning me about digging up ghosts. Do you know something you're not telling me?"

He shrugged and asked, "Why would I?"

"Maybe these attempts of violence against me might have more to do with a jealous ex-husband than the story I'm researching."

Cathy's eyebrows shot up, and turned and looked at Jerry. "Is he right? Have you been following us around, Jerry?"

Jerry snorted. "I'm over you, Cathy. Besides, if I were the jealous type, I'd have kicked Ricky's ass by now."

Cathy sneered. "As if you could."

Bill cleared his throat. "I love family reunions as much as anyone, but I think we should call it a night."

Jerry glowered at Bill. Bill's guess was that Jerry was very much the jealous type. It takes one to know one. He didn't know if he was the type to follow Cathy and him around or make lame attempts on their lives.

"I'll let you lock up, Jerry," Cathy said with sugary sweetness. "Have a nice evening."

Outside Bill said, "Ricky was right about you."

"Really? What did he say?"

"He said you were dangerous."

Cathy just laughed.

The next morning Bill had breakfast at the Dairy Queen. It wasn't as good as the Blue Bonnet, but it kept Bill from encountering Cathy. She had been a big help, but she had become a distraction.

After breakfast, Bill called Valerie to tell her that he was going to pack up and come home.

"Did you find out what happened to the girl?"

"No," Bill said, "but I've managed to piss off someone. I don't think there is a good enough story here to risk my life."

"Why do I think this has more to do with that cute little reporter from the local paper?"

Bill sighed. "Because it does," he said. "Cathy's been very helpful, but..."

"She wants to sleep with you."

"Yeah, I think she might."

"Do you want to sleep with her?"

"I wouldn't find the prospect disgusting, but I've resisted. I love you, Valerie. I don't want to mess up what we have. Any more than it has been."

"Where have I heard those words before? Oh, I remember. It's the same thing I tell you every time you get agitated when I speak to another man."

Bill felt genuinely ashamed. He didn't like the feeling of being suspected of infidelity, and he had probably come closer to doing it than Valerie ever had. What an idiot he'd been.

"I'm sorry, Valerie," Bill said. "I'm coming home."

"As your wife, I want to say 'get your ass home,' but I'm also your business partner. We need a story out of this, and I think there is one. If the shoe were on the other foot, I'd be flirting with every man I encountered to get from them what I could. That's probably what Cathy is doing. I say keep your pecker in your pants, but play her. Let her think you might give her a tumble. See what you can get from her."

Bill told her what happened in the hotel room. He expected her to get really angry, but was surprised to find her rather calm about it.

"You see?" she said. "You can do this. You did the professional thing and got the picture of the tattoo. Can you send it to me?"

"Yeah, I guess. There's WIFI here, but it doesn't reach this room. I have to pay extra, but I can connect in the lobby. I haven't even unpacked my laptop. Maybe I'll just go borrow Cathy's computer."

"Give it another day, Bill. I still think you're onto something."

"I'm sorry. I know you are right, but I just don't think the story is worth all this," he said with a sigh.

"Maybe not, but you've not exhausted all the leads yet.

Finish the job."

Bill walked over to the courthouse and around to the back where he found the sheriff's office. There was access to the office through the courthouse, but Bill wanted to avoid Chuck. As he walked in the door, a severe looking Latina woman in a uniform stepped in front of him. "You're not supposed to come through this door. It is for employees only," she said.

"I apologize. But there was no sign outside to that effect. It just said, 'Sheriff's Office.' I want to see the sheriff."

"Well, if you want to see the sheriff, you have to come in through the right door."

I pointed to the door just behind her. "Isn't that the door?"

"Yes, it is."

"Couldn't I just walk around your desk then it would be like I came through that door?"

"We have rules for a reason. You have to go around and come in the correct door."

Bill, in hindsight, realized that if he would have been smarter, he would have walked around the building as she had asked, but instead he asked, "What possible reason could you have for making me go all the way around to the front of the courthouse, when you could take care of my needs right here and right now?"

"Sir, this is my last warning. Please go around and come through the other door."

"Warning? What are you going to do if I don't?" Bill asked.

She pulled out a small can of pepper spray and sprayed

it directly into his eyes. There was a blood-curdling scream that Bill soon realized was his, and as he covered his burning eyes with his hands, he heard Ricky's voice. "Leticia! What the hell?"

"He came in the wrong door," Leticia said, calmly.

A few minutes later Bill sat in Ricky's office with a towel filled with ice applied to his eyes. It was still burning, but the ice made it bearable. "I'm sorry about that," Ricky said. "Leticia gets a little intense about the rules."

"I'm glad you don't let her have a gun."

"Actually, she does have a gun, but I don't think she would have shot you because of the door issue. She might have if you'd tried to use the copier, though. What are you doing here?"

Bill tried to look up, but his eyes couldn't focus. He just put the ice pack back on them. "I wanted to talk to you about what happened to Cathy and me outside of Kerrville."

"What happened?"

Bill told him about the spike strip blowing out the tires on his rental car.

"I don't have one of those," Ricky said. "There are just too many liability issues in using those things. Some of the earlier sheriffs had them, but I don't. Let me go call the people up in Kerrville and see what they have discovered. Keep that ice on your eyes. It should quit burning in another forty minutes or so. Tonight, when you shower hold your head back so the spray will wash away from your eyes. Otherwise, the burning will start again from the spray that's still in your hair."

It was more than an hour before it quit burning enough so Bill could see, and Ricky hadn't returned. He started looking at the pictures and certificates on the wall behind his desk. He was little surprised to see that Ricky had a master's degree in criminal justice from Sam Houston University. Suddenly, something caught his eye that surprised him even more. He stood and walked over to get a better look at the certificate. He pulled out his notebook and made a note. Ricky walked back in and Bill flipped the notebook shut.

"A lot of hard work went into getting that piece of paper," Ricky said, as he walked to his desk. "And no one around here gives a shit."

"Well, I'm impressed," Bill said. "I'm sure your parents were really proud."

"My mother was. I never met my biological father, but I think my adoptive father was proud of me, too."

"Cathy said they were both Mexican nationals."

He laughed. "My mother was born here, but her parents were undocumented. They still call them 'wetbacks' here. They got deported, but my mother stayed here."

Bill started to ask one more question, but he was thought Ricky would just lie to him, and he didn't want to show his hand just yet. He needed more information. "What did you find out from Kerrville?"

"The spike strip was police issue, but the serial number had been filed off. It must've been stolen."

"Do you think the guy who put it there was after me?"

"It does seem coincidental, but why do you think anyone around here would want to hurt you?"

"I haven't really been welcomed with open arms here. Chuck seems to hate me, and you ran me out of the courthouse. Cathy's ex-husband thinks I've slept with her, or that I'm going to. I think Cathy is irritated with me because I haven't slept with her. And, for the record, your receptionist just pepper sprayed me. So, I'm apparently an annoyance to everyone."

Ricky laughed and said, "Okay, we've been less than hospitable, but I don't think any of those people want to kill you."

"Well, I have one more person I want to speak to. And

if he doesn't try and strangle me with a rosary, I'll probably pack up and head for home tomorrow."

"You're going to speak to Father Gomez?" Ricky asked.

"Yes," Bill said. "How'd you know?"

"He was my priest when I lived in Forester. I figured you'd go to him eventually."

"You didn't tell me you lived in Forester."

Ricky leaned back in his chair and put his boots up on his desk and his hands behind his head. "I was born there, in your old house, as a matter of fact."

"Your parents bought that old house?"

He laughed and said, "I don't know if they ever bought it, but they lived there. I was born in that house, though."

"Small world," Bill said. "Why didn't you tell me that earlier?"

"I'm not sure why I am telling you now. I still don't know if I can trust you."

Bill didn't trust him, either, because now he thought he knew what Ricky was hiding.

CHAPTER 14

Bill had tried to call, but Ricky had told him that if Father Gomez didn't have his hearing aid in, he wouldn't hear the phone.

"Won't that mean he won't hear me knocking, either?" Bill asked.

"He'll see you coming," Ricky said. "If I know Father Gomez, he'll be sitting on his front porch when you get there."

"Is that where he spends most of his time?"

"No, he doesn't. He just seems to know when he's going to have company. Maybe God tells him. I don't know, but he's always waiting for me when I go to visit him."

"How often do you visit him," Bill asked, "and why?"

Ricky didn't answer.

The little white cottage where Father Gomez lived was small, but he had a nice neatly trimmed yard. The sheriff had been right. The old priest was on the porch. He smiled pleasantly at Bill as he walked up the little walk. Despite the sweltering heat, the old man sat in a lawn chair with a serape draped across his legs.

"Father Gomez," Bill said, loudly. "I am Bill Clark, a reporter from a paper in New Mexico. I wonder if I could ask you some questions."

"I have my hearing aid in, so you don't have to shout," the old priest said, "also I know who you are and why you are here."

Bill assured himself that the gossip was the reason the priest knew about him, and not something more mystical.

The old man pointed to another lawn chair. Bill accepted his offer, but he was rather hoping they could go inside with some air conditioning. Of course, there was a good chance this old priest didn't have any air conditioning.

Fr. Gomez opened a small ice chest he had next to his chair. "May I offer you a soft drink or a beer?"

"Beer sounds good, but it's a little early. I'll take a soft drink, though."

He handed Bill a cola, but then he pulled out a long-neck bottle of beer. "It's never too early for me to drink a beer. So, what are your suspicions?"

"Can I make this in the form of a confession?"

"Are you Catholic?"

"No."

"Well, it wouldn't do any good then. You're still going to hell, or at least, purgatory," he said with a laugh.

Bill smiled. "You're probably right about that. I was just hoping for confidentiality, but I don't suppose you're obligated to do that for a backslidden Baptist."

"Unless you are going confess a crime, or something really juicy, I can keep a confidence between the two us as a gentleman."

"You won't need to keep it forever. I just don't want you to tell Ricky what I'm thinking."

He laughed and said, "I imagine he already knows, but he won't hear anything from me if you don't want me to tell him. Understand, however, that I have the same agreement with him. There is only a portion I can tell you."

"That's fair," Bill said. "You said you already know why I

am here."

He nodded. "You want to know what happened to the girl that collapsed on your porch. I suppose your mother didn't ever tell you."

"You knew my mother?" Bill asked.

"Yes. I understand you believe she passed away."

Bill's heart raced. "Do you know otherwise?"

The priest didn't answer, but just smiled. "She was a caring, compassionate woman," he said finally.

"Did you know Teresa Rosales?"

The old man's bushy eyebrows shot up. "Yes. Why do you ask?"

"Sheriff Prine thought she was the girl."

Fr. Gomez took a swig of his beer. "And now he is dead."

"You think the two things are related?"

"You said you were Baptist, but you don't believe."

Bill shrugged.

"Now who is being elusive?" the priest laughed.

"I don't really want to discuss religion."

Fr. Gomez laughed and said, "Then you probably shouldn't be talking to a priest."

"Good point. I guess I believe that there is some truth to be found in religion. I believe in the principles that Jesus taught, but I don't really believe that Samson killed ten thousand Philistines with the jawbone of an ass."

He nodded. "Let me be more specific. Do you believe in evil?"

The way he asked it sent a slight chill through Bill. He suspected the priest was going to talk about demons.

"Evil is easier to believe," Bill said. "All I have to do is turn on the news. Or I could just point to history."

"People do evil things, but that isn't what I'm talking about. Do you believe in evil as a malevolent force? A force that causes people to do evil things?"

Bill shook his head. "That sounds supernatural. I don't think I believe in supernatural. People do evil things out of greed, selfishness, or, in many cases, just plain stupidity. I think people are responsible for their own behavior, though. They can't say the devil made them do it."

He smiled and nodded his head. "Yes, that's the way I believe, usually. But something is wrong here. It's connected to that girl you saw all those years ago, and that force is still here. It might just be people doing evil things, but why they are doing evil things, I just don't know."

"Was Teresa Rosales that girl?" Bill asked, again.

"I suppose this will answer the question in some way, but I'm not at liberty to answer that question, or the next one you are about to ask."

A good reporter would ask the question anyway, but for some reason Bill decided not to. Bill was sure the old man knew the question and Bill knew he wouldn't answer it.

"Do you know what happened to that girl?"

"Yes, and your mother knew that, too. She didn't tell you what happened for the same reason I won't tell you now. She kept it from you to protect you. You still need that protection. You should pack your things and go home. The evil that was here is still here," the old man said with an intense stare.

"But it's my job to find it and expose it. Isn't that how you were trained, Padre? That you fight the darkness with light?"

"Yes, but you are wrong. It is not your job, and better

people than you have tried to expose the evil, and now they are dead."

"Are you talking about Sheriff Prine and Deputy Elkins?"

His eyes widened. "I don't know for sure how any of them died. But I believe more have died than we'll probably ever know. Powerful forces are at play."

Fr. Gomez had the answers to Bill's questions, but it was clear he wasn't going to let Bill have them. He decided not to waste any more of the old man's time, or his own. Maybe the priest was right about Bill needing to pack up and go home.

Bill went back to his motel and bought a Faytonville Gazette out of the machine in the front. In his room, Bill tossed the paper on the bed and pulled out his cell phone and dialed Valerie's number.

"How's it going?" she asked.

"Not well," Bill said. "I think I have two choices. Either I come home, or I go check out Fifth Sun."

"Yeah, about that—"

"What?"

"They won't let unescorted males go there without a background check, because it's a family resort. You also need to go with a member the first time."

"Crap."

"Just go with your reporter friend," Valerie said. "I have a feeling that she is a member."

Bill paused and said, "I'm sure she'd go, but I wanted to go undercover. If I go with her, they'll know I'm press."

"I'm sure there are other members in town. Ask around. Everyone will know. Just remember whoever you get, she can look, but she can't touch."

"It's always good to establish the ground rules in these situations," Bill said, laughing.

After Bill hung up, he decided to read the paper. Bill tended to look at other newspapers with a critical eye. He noticed typos and grammar errors that most people might overlook. Ironically, that didn't mean he never made any. If Valerie didn't proofread his work, his stories would be barely coherent. His mind tended to get ahead of his fingers.

The Faytonville Gazette looked exceptionally good for a small weekly. The ads jumped out at him, but didn't overwhelm. The pages were all set up nicely. Cathy did a good job.

Most of the stories were syndicated stories, but each page had a story bylined by Cathy. She was a good writer--clear and concise. One story caught his eye:

Ranchers Testify in Fifth Sun Reservoir Hearings

The story caught Bill's eye for many reasons. First, it interested him because it was about the nudist resort's reservoir, but second because it mentioned that the chairman of the Senate Committee on Water Policy was Senator Larry Whitman. Bill normally didn't follow Texas politics, but he'd met this man. In fact, Bill had written a story about him a few years before. He and a bunch of his fellow Democrat representatives hid in New Mexico to avoid a quorum on a vote on redistricting.

It was bad enough that the senator and his friends didn't stay in Austin and do their jobs, but this jerk went fly-fishing with their local state representative and was trying to get him to consider putting a dam on the Gila River down south of Copper City. A buddy of Bill's, who owned the sporting goods store overheard them talking about it while they were buying gear and called him. He found the two of them out wading in the river and questioned them. Bill rushed back and printed the story. The local ranchers and environmentalists read the stories and united to put a quick halt to even consideration of such a project. A couple of the ranchers threatened to hog-tie Whitman and take him back to Austin themselves.

From what Bill could tell from this story in the Gazette, the local ranchers around Forester were just as angry at Whitman as New Mexico ranchers had been back then. They felt the dam at Fifth Sun was preventing the much-needed water from getting to the ranches. Whitman had presented the legislation and twisted the arms needed to get the reservoir built when he was a representative, and now as a senator he was in control of the policies that determined how much water would be released. The senator thought everything was going smoothly but promised to look into the problem. The ranchers complained that they were suffering from the worst drought since the one back in 1947-57 decade and they needed more water released.

Bill was struck by the fact that there was no mention of what the Fifth Sun resort was. Cathy held to her word about not writing about the place. Still, Bill thought that if he were the ranchers, he'd be really pissed that his cattle were dying so a bunch of naked people could swim in a lake. He wondered what stake Whitman had in it. He knew why he hated Whitman, and it wasn't just about the Gila dam suggestion.

Bill made a mental note to ask Cathy about the story the next time he saw her. For the moment, however, he didn't think he wanted to talk to her. He looked at his watch and thought he could go to the Blue Bonnet without running into her. It was two in the afternoon, so he'd missed the lunch rush.

There were only a handful of customers in the Blue

Bonnet and they didn't even look up when Bill walked in. Bill guessed they were getting used to him. Sally, the waitress, was at Bill's table as he took a seat. "What can I get ya, hon?" she asked.

"I think I could go for another one of those chicken fried steaks," Bill said. "Sally, could I ask you a strange question?"

She shrugged and said, "I suppose so. I get lots of strange questions in this place."

"I don't want to offend you."

"Men hit on me on a daily basis. I don't get offended too easy."

"Well, my question is similar, but less personal. Do you happen to know if there is a woman here in Faytonville that has ever been to the nudist resort over in Forester?"

She laughed and said, "Well, I sure as hell haven't. I've been tempted, but I don't know anyone who has. If anyone knows it would be Charlotte."

"Charlotte Brown? The librarian?"

"If she don't know anything about something there ain't nothin' to be known."

"I wouldn't think this would be subject she'd be interested in," Bill said.

"You'd be surprised. Let me go give the cook your order."

Sally seemed like a nice girl, but Bill couldn't help but wonder. She came back with a glass of tea.

"Hey, Sally, I know I'm pushing it," Bill said. "but would you ever entertain the idea of going out to that place?"

"With you?"

"Yes. I really need a member, but I think they would be willing to make some exceptions if I offered them someone that looked like you."

She blushed, which made Bill realize that she was getting the wrong idea. "I'm sorry, Sally. I shouldn't have asked. I'm not asking for any sexual reason. They won't let an unescorted male go out there without a lengthy background check."

She laughed and said, "I see. Well, what I was going to say is that I wouldn't mind getting naked with you, but I ain't going to parade around naked in front of a bunch of strangers. Sorry."

Now it was Bill's turn to blush. "Thanks," he said.

CHAPTER 15

Bill didn't think Charlotte would misinterpret what he would be asking, but he just hoped she didn't get offended and slap him upside the head.

"How can I help you?" she asked.

"This is difficult to ask, but it's about the resort outside Forester,"

She smiled and asked, "The nudist resort?"

"Correct."

"What is it you would like to know?"

Bill took a deep breath and said, "It's really important that you tell no one about this, Charlotte."

"I will admit that I listen to gossip," Charlotte said, frowning, "but I don't spread it. Everyone knows that if they tell me something it stops with me."

Since Bill was about to ask her to share gossip, he hoped that wasn't true, and he knew it was hypocritical for him to ask her to keep his confidence. Gossip always works on a quid pro quo basis. People don't share gossip with people who will not reciprocate. "Very well," he said. "Just understand that I need to do something rather dramatic to research for my story."

She laughed and said, "You're planning to go to the resort undercover? Or more accurately, you're planning on going without cover."

"Precisely."

"But you need a female member, because they won't allow unescorted men without a thorough background check."

"You're right on the money," Bill said. "I need to know who might go with me and not freak out."

"You do know that another part of the requirement is that you have to sign a non-disclosure agreement? You won't be able to report anything you see without getting sued—or worse."

Bill frowned and asked, "What do you mean?"

She shook her head and said, "Never mind. I'm just saying that you're taking a big risk going out there. They have some powerful people involved, and they don't like reporters— especially the undercover kind."

"But if I observe something that is criminal—wait a minute. How do you know all this?"

"Simple. I'm a member," she said, "I pay an annual fee."

Bill stared at her slack-jawed. He didn't know what to say.

"It usually surprises people," she said, "but it shouldn't. There are more people out there that are my age than younger."

"It's not your age so much as it is that you don't seem the type."

"What is the type? We all get naked sometime. I'm just not so shy about it. If I could do this job naked, I would. Clothes are so restrictive. It's silly that we feel we have to be covered in this heat and humidity," she said.

"Can you take me out there?" Bill asked.

She hesitated. Bill wondered why a woman who got naked with strangers was now showing hesitation. "I can take you as my guest, and you won't have to pay. How about tomorrow? It's a state holiday. The library will be closed."

"Sure. What should I bring?"

"I usually just wear a moo-moo with nothing underneath. The less you wear, the less you have to put in the locker. They have towels available there. Oh yes, don't forget to bring sunscreen."

"Okay. Any rules I should be aware of?" he asked.

"A few. This place is all about being natural and not about sex. If you get-uh-shall we say 'excited,' you need to cover yourself with a towel until the feeling subsides. There is no public sexual activity allowed. But probably the rule most newbies have trouble with is remembering not to sit on or lean against anything metal that has been out in the sun."

Bill laughed. "I could see where that might be a problem," he said. "How about I pick you up around nine?"

"Let me pick you up instead," Charlotte replied, "You need a grill guard on your vehicle to get past the bump gate."

"What's a bump gate?" Bill asked.

"It'll be easier to show you that explain it to you. I'll show you tomorrow."

"Okay," Bill said, and turned to leave, but then thought of another question. "What's the holiday tomorrow?"

"Emancipation day," she said, with a smile. "Kind of appropriate, don't you think?"

When Bill walked out to his car, and Cathy was sitting on the hood. "What's this I hear about you looking for a woman to get naked with and you didn't ask me?" she asked.

Obviously, Sally was less discrete than she claimed.

"You were my first choice, but I needed someone who wasn't a recognized member of the press. I was afraid if I went with you, it would blow my cover. Besides, if I were with you, I would spend all day covering my, as Charlotte put it —'excitement' with a towel."

She smiled and said, "Aw, that's sweet. I forgive you. Don't be too sure, though, that you won't have the same problem with Charlotte. She's a lot hotter than most people notice. Anyway, I'll be there tomorrow just the same, but I'll pretend not to know you if it'll make you feel better."

"Why are you are going?"

She laughed and said, "I'm a member, too. And I hope you understand they'll know everything about you in an hour's time, anyway."

"Why is that?"

"Well, the gossip chain is faster out there than it is here, but you're going to have to show some identification to get in."

Bill nodded and said, "I had thought about that. I have a fake ID."

"Don't use it. It'll just get you kicked out. This place has really good security. If they suspect that your identification is fake, you'll be out of there before you can unbutton your shirt. They'll do a complete background check on you before they let you into the resort. It just gets expedited when you go with a member."

"Why is that?" Bill asked.

"It's a family resort, which means there will be children there, too. They can't take any chances with pedophiles."

"Then I guess I should just forget about being undercover then. I'll go tell Charlotte that I'll just go out there with you."

Cathy shook her head and said, "No, it'll be better for me if you go out there with Charlotte. Besides, she'd be hurt now. I'm sure she's excited about it. She's been wanting to spend some time with you."

"Why is that?" Bill asked.

Cathy shrugged and said, "I don't know. She just said

she would like to get to know you better."

As they stood there talking, Bill saw a white Chevy Silverado pick-up driving slowly past. All he could see of the driver was his red hair. "Isn't that your husband?" Bill asked.

She turned and looked at the truck. She shot him the bird with both hands. "Ex-husband, Bill. Don't forget that, and don't worry about him. He's harmless."

Bill pulled out my handkerchief and wiped his forehead. "It's hot out here. Can we go somewhere else to finish this conversation?"

"How about your motel room?" she said, and winked.

"I was thinking of the newspaper office."

She sighed. "You can't blame a girl for trying. I walked down here. My I ride with you?"

The short drive later they were sitting around her desk. She'd pulled a couple of cans of Diet Dr. Pepper out of a small refrigerator and handed Bill one. Bill popped open the can, took a drink then asked, "So what are you working on? The Whitman story?"

Her eyebrows shot up. "You've been reading my paper?" she asked.

"Yes. It's a good paper. You do a good job."

"Thanks. So, you know about Sen. Whitman?"

"Actually, I've met the man. I think he's an ass."

"Yeah," she said. "Yeah, he is."

Something about her expression struck Bill as strange.

"There was something in your story that caught my attention," Bill said.

"Really? What is that?"

"One of the ranchers said something about the drought that occurred between 1947 and 1957. Don't those dates ring a bell?"

Her eyes widened. "Those were the years that Sheriff Prine listed in his notes. Do you think there's any significance in that?"

"Could you check and see if there were any drought conditions the year the girl landed on our porch?"

Cathy turned to her computer and typed in a search. She found a site and clicked on it. She shook her head. "Ground water levels were a little low still, but it was our highest rainfall in years."

Bill shrugged. "There's no connection to droughts then," he said. "Could you check and see when Fifth Sun became a nudist resort?"

Her fingers clattered over the keys. "Huh," she said.

"What?"

"The reservoir was built in 1961 and they became a nudist colony in 1962. But it was still considered a church, too. When Jeremiah died in 1993, Jeremy dropped the church status and turned it into a resort."

"Who financed the reservoir? It seems like it's only there to benefit the resort."

"The permit was granted by the legislature, but it was funded by a grant from the Nanahuatl Foundation."

"Search that word," Bill said. "Nanahuatl sounds strange."

She typed it in. "He was an ugly Aztec god that was full of sores," she said, "and he threw himself into a fire to save the Fifth Sun, not the resort, but the actual sun."

Bill leaned back in his chair and looked up at the ceiling. Thoughts tumbled around in his brain. "I don't believe a little Aztec cult could finance a dam," he said. "Even if they could, they couldn't possibly have had that much influence on the Texas legislature. I don't care when or where they are built, dams are big deals. The environmental movement was in its infancy to be sure, but there were conservationists back then. Of course, ranchers tend to be against them. People watch these projects closely. As Mark Twain said, 'Whiskey is for drinking; water is for fighting over.'"

Cathy nodded and took a sip of her Diet Dr. Pepper. "Environmentalists aren't so loud in Texas. They're here but do everything through the courts. Tree huggers get shot if they show up on private property around here. The biggest problems with the dams are whose land gets flooded and whose property doesn't get enough of the water. Fifth Sun gets most of its grief from the cattle ranchers, because the resort raises sheep."

"Why would a nudist resort want to raise sheep?"

"It's always been a working sheep ranch and it brings in some extra income during the winter. People are not as inclined to get nude during the winter months. Before the drought and the drop in wool prices there was a lot of sheep ranching in this county. Listen, Bill, I have to run some errands. You can use the office here if you want. I'll be back around dinner time."

Bill nodded and watched her walk out the door. He did a little more research on the Aztecs but didn't find anything of any use. He went out to his car and got the SD card out of his camera. He emailed Valerie the pictures of Cathy's tattoo.

For several hours Bill just surfed the Internet, but he wasn't finding anything and was getting bored. He didn't make a habit of snooping on other people's computers, but he didn't think Cathy would mind. He clicked on her "My Pictures" file.

Cathy had just told him that she was a member of the nudist resort but was stunned when the screen filled hundreds of thumbnails of naked people. Most of them were adults, but a few of them were of a young girl who had to be in her early teens. He clicked on the icon, and the picture filled the screen. She was a lovely young girl, and Bill realized quickly that she was too young for him to be looking at. He closed the picture. He found a couple of pictures of Cathy and spent a little too much time staring at them, as well. Guilt and other feelings overwhelmed him, so he closed the pictures. There was a couch against one wall. Bill used it to take a nap and he'd been so tired Cathy had to shake him to get him awake three hours later.

"You want to go to the Blue Bonnet?" she asked.

Bill was getting a little tired of the Blue Bonnet and he wasn't really comfortable seeing Sally again. "Do you have any other suggestions?" he asked.

"I know a good Mexican food place. It's across the tracks."

In most towns in Texas, "across the tracks" means lower income and a different ethnicity. However, it almost always is where a person can find the best food.

CHAPTER 16

Cathy suggested that Bill just ride with her since she knew the way. He was reluctant, but he agreed. She had to move a big pile of papers, notebooks, and camera equipment from the passenger seat for him to get in. "Sorry about the mess," she said.

"Don't be," Bill replied, "This looks just like my Buick back home."

They drove to the north side of town and pulled up in front of what looked like someone's house, except for the big neon sign that said, "Chapo's" in the picture window.

As they entered, a cowbell above the door clattered. The place was crowded with chrome dinette sets of assorted colors and styles, but no other customers. The floor was old wood with serious need of waxing and the walls were covered with neon beer signs and a couple of Mexican flags. There was a wall between the dining room and the kitchen with a service window. Bill could see the top of someone's dark head wearing a hairnet. "That must be Chapo," Bill said, smiling.

"I'll be with you guys in a minute," the short man said. "Have a seat wherever you want."

"He's the waiter, cook, and dishwasher," Cathy said, as they took the seats at a red dinette set.

In a moment, the little man pushed through a set of swinging doors. He froze when he saw Bill, and Bill recognized him immediately. It was the man he'd seen in Kerrville by the Coke machine at the motel. "What the hell?" Bill said.

The little man recovered. "You look familiar," he said.

"Of course, I do. You were spying on us in Kerrville."

"What are you talking about, Bill?" Cathy asked.

"He was outside our motel room in Kerrville. He was pretending to buy a Coke when I went to go get us something to eat."

Cathy looked at Chapo then back at Bill and said, "Okay, that is a little strange, but why didn't you tell me?"

"I didn't want to scare you."

"I wasn't spying," Chapo said. "Well, not really. I was staying at that motel and I saw you and Cathy. I was a little curious."

"Curious about what?" Bill asked.

"About you," Chapo said. "I didn't know Cathy was seeing anyone."

"Why were you in Kerrville, Chapo?" Cathy asked.

"I know this will be hard to believe, but I was at the folk festival."

Bill laughed and said, "You're right. I do find that hard to believe. You like folk music? I would think you would prefer Mariachi."

"That's sort of racist, don't you think?" Chapo asked, angrily. "I prefer Dylan and Seeger, but for the record, Mariachi is folk music."

Bill stared at Chapo and thought the little man might be telling the truth. "Normally, I'd believe you, but someone tried to kill us when we left Kerrville," Bill said. "So, you can see why I find your curiosity a little suspicious."

Chapo's eyes widened. "Kill you? How?" he asked

"Someone blew out our tires with one of those spike strips the police use to stop high speed chases," Cathy said.

"I don't think Ricky has one of those things and he'd never let me borrow it if he did."

"I didn't mention Ricky," Bill said. "Why would we think you'd borrow anything from Ricky?"

"Chapo is Ricky's stepfather," Cathy said.

Bill's mind started turning. "That makes you even more suspect," he said. "Just curious. Where is your wife? I would like to talk to her."

"She's in Corpus Christi visiting with her sister," Chapo said. "Why do you want to speak to her?"

"Just a hunch," Bill said. "What is your wife's name?"

"Maria."

"What was her maiden name?" Bill asked.

He looked at Bill suspiciously. "Gonzales. Why?"

"Do you own a .22 rifle?" Bill asked.

"Yes, but so do most of the people in this town."

A couple of Mexican men entered the café. They looked at us for a few seconds then took a table on the other side of the room. Their eyes went a little wide from the obvious tension between Chapo and Bill.

"I'm sorry, Bill," Cathy said, "but I don't see where any of this is going. I'm hungry and you're upsetting the cook. Let's order before the dinner rush starts."

Chapo's other customers were obviously concerned. Bill nodded and Chapo took their order and headed back to the kitchen. He came back out immediately and took the order from the two men.

"What's going on, Bill?"

"He's lying."

"No, he's not. Ricky's mother's name is Maria Gonzales.

I know that for a fact. I also know that he does like folk music."

"Have you seen her birth certificate?" Bill asked.

"No."

"Then you don't know it for a fact. He's also lying about her being in Corpus Christi."

Cathy nodded and said, "On that point I think you are right. Ricky told me he didn't have any other family in the States."

"Ricky probably doesn't know the truth. I think his mother has been lying to him from the day he was born."

"Who do you think Ricky's mother is?"

Bill started to tell her, but decided to keep it to himself. He didn't really have any proof. Besides, Cathy continues to show him that she has a lot of information that she won't volunteer. "Never mind," Bill said. "I'm jumping to conclusions. Let's see what happens tomorrow."

Chapo brought out their food and they ate it in silence. Cathy got chili rellenos and Bill got a combination plate. New Mexico has great Mexican food, but this beat anything Bill had ever eaten. Bill just hoped it hadn't been seasoned with rat poison.

After dinner, Cathy invited Bill to her house, but he refused her invitation.

"C'mon, Bill. There's no reason for you to hang around in that cheap hotel room. I have a big screen television and lots of beer."

"That sounds good, but I think I need some time to think."

"You're going to be thinking about your trip to the nudist resort. If you want a practice run, I have a six-foot fence in my backyard. I could invite over a few of my nudist friends. You can get used to being naked and have a few Coronas."

Bill wasn't worried about public nudity, although his body wasn't what it used to be. He did have some concerns about being naked with Cathy under any circumstances. "I'll see you tomorrow, Cathy." he said, and went back to the Motel Six.

Charlotte was waiting for him in the lobby, early the next morning. He hadn't been able to sleep and was up early doing as much grooming as possible. He didn't do any shaving or waxing, but for the first time in his life he wished he could have. He was young and almost hairless the last time he got naked in public. The hair on his back bothered him, but he couldn't do anything about it at this point.

As she had said, Charlotte was wearing a thin moo-moo and obviously nothing else. Bill wore a pair of shorts and a t-shirt. He had bought a pair of cheap slip-on sandals the clerk called "thongs" and sunscreen. Charlotte gave Bill an approving nod. "Those shorts leave little to the imagination," she said. "You're wise to go without underwear, but you will need your ID."

Bill pulled up his shirt and showed her his driver's license tucked in his waistband.

"That'll work," she said. "Did you bring sunscreen?"

Bill showed her the bottle in his hand. "I've already applied some, but I was wondering about how I would go about applying more when I got there."

She laughed and said, "The guys do it several ways. The newbies usually do the vital areas under a towel. After a while most men are able to apply it without a reaction. Hell, some men can let someone else apply it without a reaction."

Bill shuddered and said, "I hope I never get to that point."

Bill got in the car and soon they were on the road in Charlotte's large Mercury with the grill guard on front. Charlotte smoked, but Bill didn't complain. It was her car. He remembered the trips his family used to take as a kid. His mother had smoked.

"How's your story coming?" Charlotte asked after they were a few miles down the road.

"I'm not yet sure there is a story," Bill said. "Oh, I'll end up writing something, but I think the mystery of the girl on my porch may be a disappointment. There are some strange things going on around here, but I'm not sure it has anything to do with that girl."

"I don't know what to tell you," she said. "I doubt if you'll find out anything about the girl at Fifth Sun, but you'll definitely find something of interest."

"What do you know about Jeremy Porter?" Bill asked.

"Not much. He inherited the ranch from his father and turned it into the nudist resort. His father had manipulated the land away from the Aztec cult years ago and turned it into his own cult. Jeremy didn't buy into the religious aspects."

"His father was Jeremiah Ray?"

She nodded. "A real bastard, I've heard. If he hadn't died when he did, he would have probably turned the place into another Waco situation."

Bill shook his head, and said, "It's amazing to me that I can't talk my way out of a traffic ticket, but some men are able to convince a crowd of intelligent people to drop everything and follow them into total obedience."

"I think that's why Jeremiah kept the sheep on the ranch," Charlotte said. "He liked the symbolism. Most people are like sheep. They'll follow the lead sheep off a cliff if that's where it goes."

"So, Jeremy didn't inherit that ability?" Bill asked.

She laughed and said, "No. I wouldn't follow Jeremy out

of a burning building. He's a nice guy, but far from charismatic. The nudist resort idea was probably a way to keep the naked people coming. No one's ever seen him with a partner, male or female. He has a daughter, but that seems suspicious, too."

"Why is that?" Bill asked.

"What kind of mother lets her teenage girl stay with a nudist father?"

"I agree. I consider myself a libertarian. I think consenting adults ought to be able to do as they please, but I have a totally different attitude about children. They are completely at the mercy of adults. They need to be protected."

That statement caused Charlotte some obvious discomfort. "That sounds a little personal," she said.

"I suppose. I always felt a little vulnerable after my mom left me. I know my dad could be a jerk, but why did she leave me?"

"Sometimes leaving a child is the best thing for the child."

Bill turned and looked at Charlotte. "I'm sorry," Bill said. "Did I hit a nerve?"

"Yes, but I don't want to talk about it. But as a reporter you know you shouldn't run a story without all the facts. I don't think you have all the facts."

"Yes, ma'am," Bill said.

She laughed. "It seems that your mama taught you some manners before she left."

Charlotte drove a lot slower than the sheriff had, but the trip went by quickly, even though they went the rest of the way in an awkward silence. Before Bill knew it, they were pulling up to the gate at Fifth Sun. A small rush of adrenaline ran through his veins.

Charlotte pressed a button on a little metal speaker box. A tinny voice squawked something Bill couldn't make out. Charlotte gave her name and a member number. There was a pause and there was the whirring of an electrical motor as the first gate opened slowly. She drove into the sally port and the first gate closed. A moment passed and the next gate opened. They began following a very narrow, a road through an orchard of pecan trees.

"Pecan trees usually need lots of water," Bill said. "These seem to be flourishing."

"All thanks to the dam on the Frio," Charlotte replied

They drove about a mile and came to a six-foot solid wood gate that was hanging from steel cables attached to a tall steel pole in the middle. "This is the bump gate I was telling you about," Charlotte said.

She drove right up to the gate and put the grill right against it. She gunned the motor, pushing the gate open and sped through with the back part of the gate almost hitting the rear of the car. "You have to time things just right," she said, "or you'll tear the shit out of your car."

"What's the deal with this kind of gate?" Bill asked.

"It allows cars in without letting the sheep out. Sheep can jump over cattle guards which is probably what you're used to seeing."

They were traveling through a grassy meadow and sheep were everywhere. Charlotte had to drive slowly as the sheep lazily cleared a path for them. Soon they were parking in a big lot full of cars. In the distance Bill could see the lake. There were nude bodies, but they were too far away for him to distinguish features.

They got out of the car and approached a building Bill assumed was the office. A large naked man with red hair was standing in front of the building with his hands on his hips.

"Good morning, Charlotte," he said. "I suppose this is Mr. Clark."

"Yes," she said. "Bill, this is Jeremy Porter."

"We've been expecting you, Mr. Clark," Jeremy said. "Please come in for a brief orientation. It won't take long."

Bill supposed he should have known that he wouldn't be able to come out here without Porter being warned by someone. He had asked Charlotte not to tell Porter anything, but he figured Cathy had already filled the man in.

"I only gave him your name and address," Charlotte said. "They have to do a background check. I didn't tell him anything else."

They followed Porter into a small office. Bill was rather glad when he sat behind a large oak desk. "I notice, Mr. Clark that you work for a small newspaper. Are you here to do a story?"

"Yes sir," Bill said, "but not about Fifth Sun. I'm researching something that occurred a long time ago. There may be a possible connection to Fifth Sun before you turned it into a resort. I really have nothing to base that on. I'm talking about a summer forty years ago."

Porter nodded. "That was when my father first got here. It was a different place back then. I doubt if there is anything to be gained by your visit, but you're more than welcome here. I do need for you to sign a non-disclosure agreement. If you do write anything about us, then I will have to approve it."

"I understand."

Porter gave Bill a brief history of the nudist resort, and then went over all the rules, most of which, Charlotte had already mentioned. She hadn't mentioned the cell phone restriction, but Bill didn't bring his. He knew he wasn't going to have any place to keep it, and he didn't want to carry it around in his hand.

"Will you be spending the night?" Porter asked.

"I didn't plan to," Bill said.

"You definitely should. We won't charge you. Charlotte's bungalow has two rooms. Would that be alright, Charlotte?"

"Sure," she said, shrugging. "I wasn't planning on staying the night, but what do you say, Bill?"

"I didn't pack for overnight."

Porter laughed and said, "Not much reason to pack for a nudist resort. We have toiletries available for you to use."

Bill shrugged and said, "Why not?"

Bill didn't know why he said that, though, because he was rather certain it was the last thing he wanted to do.

CHAPTER 17

After all the papers were signed, Jeremy Porter stood and clapped his hands together. "Okay, then," he said. "Time to get nude. Charlotte will show you to the dressing room—or more accurately, the undressing room. I will be available this evening if you have further questions."

Charlotte and Bill walked out of the office and around to the back of the building. Bill was beginning to feel that he was going to endure this humiliation for nothing, but he was past the point of no return. Charlotte opened a door and he followed her into a large locker room.

"Is there only one?" Bill asked.

"Do you really think there is a need for two?" she asked. "Just find a locker that doesn't have anything in it and put your clothes in there."

Without further discussion she pulled her moo-moo over her head and threw it into an empty locker. Bill didn't mean to stare, but the sight was rather awesome. The effect was much like one of those pictures at a carnival where a person sticks her head through a hole, and it puts his or her head on a different body. He didn't know how old Charlotte was, but he didn't think she should have a body that looked that young. She sees him staring, and, to his surprise, blushes. "Not bad, huh?" she said.

Bill pulled off his shirt then dropped his shorts. Charlotte glanced at him and asked, "You ready? There's a shower back there. Some guys like to take a cold shower before leaving, but I don't really recommend it."

Charlotte grabbed a couple of towels off the shelf and tossed Bill one of them. She opened the door and walked out. Reluctantly, Bill followed and stepped out into the sun. Fortunately, there were not a lot of people out and about. There was an elderly couple sitting under the umbrella of a patio table by a small kidney shaped pool. They were eating breakfast and they didn't even glance up at Charlotte and Bill.

"Let me give you a tour," Charlotte said. "This pool here is heated for those that like the water a little warmer. It doesn't get that much use, but it's nice to sit around if you want to get away from the crowd."

"How big of a crowd are we talking about?" Bill asked.

"On the average summer day there will be a couple of hundred people here, but since this is a holiday, it can get up to three hundred."

At the opposite side of the pool was a six-foot retaining wall. In middle of the wall was a set of steps. Charlotte walked towards those steps and Bill followed. The butterflies in his stomach were subsiding a little, but when he reached the top of the stairs they came rushing back. Everywhere he looked were naked bodies.

From this vantage point, he could see the lake and the dam. The lake was surrounded by huge trees. On the east side of the lake were all the bungalows for the overnight guests and a small RV park was behind the bungalows. There was a group of people were playing volleyball, but most of the people were sitting on towels reading or chatting with each other on grassy hill.

"There's an Olympic sized pool over that ridge," Charlotte said, "but right here is where the majority of the people hang out. Next to that pool is a snack bar. They don't sell alcoholic beverages here at the resort, but lots of people bring their own coolers full of beer. They are usually more than willing to share."

Bill was feeling very naked, but after a few deep breaths, he realized that no one was looking at him. "What do you want to do?" Charlotte asked.

"I think that I would like to go sit down on the grass for a few minutes."

"Would you mind going alone? I see some friends I'd like to speak to over at the boat docks."

Bill nodded. "You have more than done your part," he said. "You needn't babysit me all day."

She laughed and shook her head. Bill wondered what she found funny about that. She said, "I'll find you at dinner. And then I'll show you where my bungalow is."

Bill watched her walk gracefully away. With the towel dangling in front of him Bill walked over to a spot on the grass that was not too close to anyone else. He had his back to the majority of the people as he spread out his towel then sat down on it in a cross-legged position.

Being careful not to stare at any one person Bill glanced around at the nude bodies around him. Most of them were adults. Very few of them seemed to be under fifty years of age. None of them seemed to be the least interested in Bill and he began to relax. He knew that if he were to find out any useful information, he was going to need to engage some of the other people in conversation, but he thought he needed to acclimate for a while.

Feeling increasingly more confident, Bill stretched out his legs and leaned back on his hands. He looked down at himself. It was a little jarring to see his naked body in such bright sunlight.

"You must be new," a female voice said. Bill looked up at a young girl, probably no more than seventeen staring down at him. She was a vision of loveliness with long brown hair and dark brown eyes. Her face was very youthful, but her body

108

seemed a little older. He thought she looked familiar, and then he realized that she was the young girl he'd seen on Cathy's computer.

"How did you know?" Bill asked.

"You aren't looking at anyone else and you are staring at your own privates like you've never seen them before. It's what all the first timers do—or more accurately what the male first-timers do. The women don't dare to look at their own bodies."

"No offense, but I thought the minors were supposed to stay close to their parents," Bill said.

"That's true, but I'm an exception," she said. "My father is Jeremy Porter. He gives me a little more leeway. My name is Madison." She extended her hand.

Bill took her hand and tried hard to maintain eye contact. "It's nice to meet you, Madison," Bill said, "but I'm sure your father doesn't want you talking to strange naked men-- especially me."

"I've rarely spoken to any men that weren't naked and if my father didn't want me talking to you, he wouldn't have told me to come over and help you feel more comfortable."

Bill went back to his cross-legged position. "It's not really working."

She plopped down next to him. "You're hung up on a set of rules that I've never experienced. If I were clothed, you wouldn't have trouble talking to me. Why does my being naked make so much of a difference? I'm not here to flirt with you and my nudity doesn't mean that I am willing to have sex with you. You are here to do a job, right? Just do it and forget that we are naked. Just talk to me like I'm a clothed person."

Bill laughed. "I'm not so sure I'd be that comfortable talking to you if you were clothed, but what do you want to talk about?"

She smiled, wickedly, and said, "You have a very nice penis."

Bill laughed again. "I like you, Madison. You are making me feel more comfortable. Have you been a nudist all your life?" he asked.

"I don't like labels. I was raised to rarely wear clothes. I put them on to go to San Antonio, but I'm probably as uncomfortable wearing clothes as you are being naked."

"So, it has nothing to do with a philosophy or belief system?"

"No. My dad has rationales for our lifestyle, but I've never given it much thought. I plan to go to college someday, so I'll probably get used to the textile world. I'll still try to be naked as much as possible, though. I imagine I'll make my roommate really uncomfortable."

"Could I ask you about your grandfather?" Bill asked.

She shrugged and said, "I didn't really know him. He died before I was born. I've seen videos of him preaching really long sermons. Mostly hellfire and brimstone stuff. I don't know why anybody like listening to that stuff."

"Really? Do you remember any specifics?"

"Not really. I just remember he ranted and raved about sin and Jesus. Sex was of the devil, except for procreation, but the nudity was purity."

"Jesus? I thought this was an Aztec cult," Bill said.

She smiled. "You've done your homework, Mr. Clark. Yes, when my grandfather first came out here it was an Aztec cult, but he came to convert them to Christianity."

"Apparently, I didn't do enough homework. I didn't know your grandfather was a Christian. Why didn't he have a problem with the nudism?"

"I don't know why, but from what my father tells me,

Granddad started the nudity."

This was a first. Charismatic cult leaders have always been good at charming people into following blindly, but this is the first time Bill had heard of someone convincing their followers to become nudists. "How did he justify that?"

"It was pretty straight forward. He got the idea from the Bible. His thinking was that since Adam and Eve were naked in the garden before they sinned that when Jesus died for our sins, we ought to be able to go back to being naked."

Bill smiled and said "There's sort of a strange logic to that."

"Yeah, but Dad thinks Granddad just wanted to see boobies. He was a pervert."

"Did he ever do more than just look?"

"That's the rumor, but my father denies it. My grandmother left my grandfather as soon as he started talking about the naked stuff. She moved to Houston and we visit her now and then, but she never comes here. She thinks we're all going to hell."

Madison seemed bright and levelheaded. "What about your mother, Madison? Is she here?"

"My father said she was a nudist, but she's not with my father anymore. She lives up in Mineral Wells."

"Why aren't you with her?"

She shrugged and leaned back on her elbows. "I don't know," she said. "She left and didn't take me with her. I've never really known her, so I don't give it much thought. Does that make sense?"

"Perfectly," Bill said, a little sadly. "I understand how you feel."

"Your mother left you?"

Bill nodded. "I didn't think much of it either until my therapist told me she thought I should. She says I have abandonment issues," he said.

"Do you like softball?" Madison asked, abruptly changing the subject.

"Yeah."

Madison stood and said, "Looks to me that you've become pretty relaxed, so my job's done. I'll be seeing you around, I'm sure. We have a softball tournament this afternoon. Do you play?"

"No. Not since high school. I bet there isn't much sliding into home plate around here, though."

She laughed and said, "No, that's true, but you might find it fun to watch."

"I have no doubt."

She turned and walked away. Bill noticed she had the same sun tattoo on her back that Cathy had on her thigh. Coincidentally, he saw Cathy walking towards him. He reached down for his towel.

CHAPTER 18

Cathy smiled as she did a brief check of Bill's naked body. "Well, that was worth waiting for," she said. "You have a rather nice body, Mr. Clark."

"Thanks," Bill replied. "So, do you, but I've already seen it."

"So how do you like being a nudist?"

"I like what Madison said. I'm just a guy without clothes. I'm not a nudist."

She smiled and said, "Ah, yes. Young Madison is rather impressive, isn't she?"

"She's a smart kid. I like her."

Cathy nodded. "Not too much, I hope."

"No, I think I much prefer women closer to my own age. Are you here with a date?"

"Sort of," she said, standing. "Do you want to meet him?"

"Sure, why not?"

Bill followed her up a grassy hill and a snack bar surrounded by patio tables came into sight. They headed for a table where a man was sitting and sipping on what appeared to be a fountain drink. Bill recognized him immediately.

"Bill, this is Senator Whitman," Cathy said, as they reached the table.

Sen. Whitman's eyes widened as he recognized Bill. "Oh shit," he said.

"Relax, I'm not here to report on you," Bill said, "or punch you in the nose, though the latter might still be an option later. How do you keep your constituents from knowing about your extracurricular activities?"

The man shrugged. "I'm sure they have heard rumors, but as long as nothing hits the papers, they won't care. If it does hit your paper, I'll be suing you for everything you own," Whitman said. "I might even be able to lure away that hot little wife of yours."

Cathy's face went a little red. "I know you told me that you'd met, Bill," Cathy said, "but it sounds like you guys know each other better than you implied."

Valerie had done most of the reporting on the story of when Sen. Whitman was a refugee in New Mexico. He'd hit on Valerie the whole time she interviewed him. Bill believed Valerie when she said they had not had a fling, but he knew that Valerie had been a little flattered by politician's ovations. Bill almost punched the man at one point, but he wasn't going to share any of that with Cathy.

"Have a seat, Bill," Whitman said. "Catch me up on the big world of Copper City, New Mexico."

Bill took a seat, not to be social, but to feel less vulnerable. "Well, we still don't have a dam on the Gila. Was this your first one?" he asked, pointing to the dam.

"I was still in high school when this one was built," he said. "Of course, I have to fight to protect it every time there's a drought in the area."

"How often is that?"

"We only have big ones here every twenty years or so. We're in one now as a matter of fact. But every spring, the ranchers think the rain isn't going to come. They can complain all they want, but I'll see all the schools are closed in this state before I let them touch this place."

Bill knew that the senator was being so forthcoming because of the non-disclosure agreement. Bill had read it carefully, and unless Bill witnessed the senator commit a major felony, Bill couldn't print a word. "So how long have you been a member of the Fifth Sun Resort?" Bill asked.

"My parents were founding members. They came here with Jeremiah."

"Actually, I thought the Aztec cult were the founding members — and owners."

Whitman laughed and said, "Those were all wetbacks. They were here illegally. They didn't own Jack."

"Jeremiah your parents the right to do what you did," Bill said. "Did you know Teresa Rosales?"

Color drained from the man's face, but he recovered quickly, as most politicians do. "Cathy told me about your story. Yes, I did know her. She was part of the cult. But that was before the nudity began here. There wouldn't have been any reason for her to have been naked, and you really don't know if it was actually Teresa that collapsed on your front porch."

"You don't think it was Teresa?" Bill asked.

"Teresa was deported before then," he said. "If Teresa is still alive today, she's in Mexico."

"I'm curious. Why was she deported and why you would know that? I heard her parents were deported, but she was actually born here, so she shouldn't have been taken taken."

The senator shrugged. "It's a matter of record. You can look it up."

"True, but I think you're wrong about where she is. I don't think she's in Mexico. In fact, I think she's living in Faytonville."

Cathy didn't flinch. Sen. Whitman, on the other hand, looked a little ill. "That's not possible," he said.

"I haven't found her, yet, but I have some information, though not completely reliable, that Teresa Rosales is still around."

"What kind of information?" Whitman asked.

"I don't want to say just yet," Bill said. "I'm sure Cathy has told you that there have been two attempts on our lives."

"The gunshots, maybe, but spike strips are designed to slow people down and not hurt anyone. Why do you think someone would try to kill you?"

"That's a good question. I'm hoping to find that out. Of course, since Cathy was with me both times, it could have been that they were trying to kill her, and not me," Bill said.

"Or maybe both of us," Cathy said.

"Or neither of you," the senator said. "You newspaper people find conspiracies in everything. You had two unfortunate mishaps. They could be pure coincidences. Why do you guys have to make everything into Watergate?"

His smug expression irritated Bill, but he knew the bravado was for show. He had the senator on the ropes. "You are making a sweeping generalization," Bill said, "like me saying all politicians are liars and crooks."

Blood rushed to the man's face. He stood. "I'm getting hot. How about a swim, Cathy?"

Cathy shrugged and looked over at Bill and asked, "Join us?"

"No thanks," Bill said. "Maybe later."

They walked away and Madison came walking over to Bill. "That didn't look like it went very well," she said.

"A little tense, indeed," Bill said, "but that's how I wanted it. If I weren't naked, I would have liked for him to take a poke at me, but I wouldn't want to fight like this."

She sat down next to Bill and said, "Dad says that if everyone was naked, there wouldn't be any wars."

"They would be pretty limited, for sure," Bill said. "Where would people keep the extra bullets? Still, naked aboriginal people in the past have found ways to fight."

She laughed with an infectious lilting laugh, but then she frowned and asked, "how do you know the senator?"

"We've met, but I don't really know him."

"He's a major prick," she said.

Bill glanced over at the senator as he was about to dive off the diving board. "You're obviously speaking metaphorically, but I know what you mean."

She laughed, again. "I like you, Mr. Clark."

"Call me Bill."

"Okay. I like you, Bill."

"I like you, too, Madison."

Before lunch, Bill decided to go back up to the locker room. Cathy caught up with him. "Where you headed?" she asked.

"I thought I'd better put on some more sunscreen."

"Can I help?"

"I'm really only planning on putting it on the parts I can reach myself."

"It's more fun if someone else puts it on."

"I have no doubt," he said, then change the subject, "What's the deal with you and Whitman?"

She smiled and asked, "Are you jealous?"

"No, but I hate to see you with someone like him."

She sighed and said, "I can't tell you what is going on

with us, but no matter what you see I want you to know it's only some personal business. There isn't any romance. I'm playing him for information."

"I have no right to interfere with your relationships, but my wife told me to do the same with you."

"I think I would like your wife. Bill, I want your respect. This just business. No matter what happens. Please remember that. I need you to trust me. You need to trust me," she said, turned, and walked away. Bill watched her. He wanted to trust her, but he really wasn't sure he could. He really couldn't think of a reason he should.

Bill didn't speak to Cathy the rest of the day. Everywhere she went she was on Whitman's arm. Bill had his fill of Whitman a long time ago. After he'd reapplied the lotion, he decided to get something to eat at the snack bar. He laughed out loud when he got a burger and headed for one of the patio tables and saw his old buddy, Chuck Tremaine.

Chuck looked up and said, "Jesus Christ, can I not go anywhere without running into you?"

Bill now understood why Chuck had the heavy-duty grill guard on his truck. "I wasn't expecting you either," he said.

He looked up and down Bill's body and his eyebrows went up. "Would you like to join me?" he asked.

"I thought you preferred to be alone."

"That was before I knew you were so--gifted."

"I'm not gay," Bill said. "Not even curious. But I would like to join you." Bill sat down across from him, thankful for the cover of the plastic table. "How long have you been coming out here, Chuck?"

"My lover, Frankie and I were long time members out here. Many of the men out here are gay."

"What about the unescorted male rule?"

"That only applies to first-time visits."

Bill had never been homophobic and he'd heard that gay men liked to frequent such resorts. "You told me Frankie had died," Bill said. "What happened?"

"It wasn't AIDS, if that was what you are thinking."

It wasn't what Bill was thinking, but denial always sounds defensive. "What was it, then?"

"I think he was sacrificed."

"What?"

"You know, put on an altar and sliced open."

Bill sat there stunned. He couldn't believe what he was hearing. His mouth was hanging open and he could see that Chuck was pleased at his reaction.

"They said he was murdered," Chuck said, "because he'd hit on the wrong guy at some bar, but Frankie didn't hit on guys. He was shy. He waited for guys to hit on him."

Bill doubted that shy people frequented nudist resorts, but he didn't want to interrupt Chuck's story.

"He joined Jeremiah's cult during the sixties, but he was still in the closet. He really liked the idea of getting naked for Jesus. I met him at the Blue Bonnet around that time, but that's when we discovered that Jeremiah was homophobic. He called us sodomites and tried to kick us out. Jeremy took up for us, but I think Jeremiah's henchmen killed Frankie."

"Why do you think that?" Bill asked. "Is there any evidence to suggest it?"

"It was all covered up. I had no rights as his lover, so I wasn't told anything. He was supposed to have been murdered in San Antonio. They found his body in an alley behind a redneck bar. The newspaper said his nuts were cut off and that he'd been gutted like a fish, but I didn't believe that."

"Didn't they do an autopsy?" Bill asked.

"Yes, but no one would let me see it. I tried for years to get a copy. Finally, I forged a deputy's signature and was able to get a copy of the autopsy sent to the courthouse."

"Was it Cathy's father? Did you forge Cathy's father's signature?"

He looked stunned and asked, "How could you possibly know that? Did Cathy tell you?"

Bill shook his head. "I didn't know, but I'm always looking for connections. Did he find out? I mean did Cathy's father find out you forged his name to get the files," he asked

"Yes, and he was pissed. He threatened to arrest me, but I convinced him to look at the autopsy. He looked at it and his face went pale. 'I'll look into this, Chuck,' he said, and I never saw him or the file again. I don't think he killed himself."

"You didn't make a copy?" Bill asked.

"I know this will be hard to believe, but we didn't even have a copier back then. The Gazette doubled as a copier service. If I wanted copies, I would have had to take it to Cathy and let her make the copies for me. You can't trust that bitch. I hope you've come to realize that."

Bill looked over at her and saw her hanging on Whitman's every word. "The jury is still out for now," Bill said. "What did the autopsy report say?"

"Frankie's abdomen had been sliced open and his heart had been removed. The coroner thought the genitalia had been cut off post-mortem. It sounded exactly like an Aztec human sacrifice."

"Okay, considering the history of this place I can see why you would think that, but I thought Jeremiah was a Christian and stopped all the Aztec beliefs."

"Jeremiah was not a Christian. He was a sociopath. He really didn't give a shit about religion at all. All he wanted was to be surrounded by young naked bodies. I think he preferred the boys, too."

"But you said he was homophobic," Bill said.

"Homophobia has changed its meaning from its original use. Psychologists first introduced the idea as 'internalized homophobia.' It originally meant a person's self-loathing for his own latent homosexuality. Jeremiah was a flaming queen in denial. He covered it up with all the religious shit. My guess is that he and Frankie had a fling and Frankie threatened to out him."

Things were getting interesting, but suddenly Madison appeared. "My dad said that he had some time, if you'd like to interview him now,"

Bill looked at Chuck. "Does Jeremy know what you suspect?" Bill asked.

"Yes. He completely agrees with me. He's been very supportive."

"So, you don't mind me questioning him about this?"

"Not at all."

Bill excused himself and followed Madison to the table where Jeremy was sitting. He smiled, stood, and shook Bill's hand. "Welcome. Have a seat."

Bill sat down and Madison walked away.

"I see you've been talking to Chuck."

Bill nodded.

"I hope you don't believe anything that crazy old queen has been telling you."

CHAPTER 19

One of the fun things about being a reporter is when stories contradict. One person thinks another person is their loyal friend, when, in fact, the other person loathes them. Jeremy's statement didn't really surprise Bill, but for the fact that he was being so openly homophobic to a reporter when his income was dependent on a large gay clientele.

"Well, he was saying some pretty nice things about you," Bill said. "He thinks you're a friend, but apparently he's being deceived."

"As long as he keeps up his membership payments, he'll be a friend," Jeremy said, "but it wouldn't bother me if he and his kind quit coming."

"According to Chuck, that would mean a large loss in revenue."

"Chuck is right, but it's something I've learned to live with. At least, I don't have to worry about them hitting on my daughter."

Bill nodded and said, "Madison is a lovely girl. If you're worried about child molesters, why do you raise her in this environment?"

"As the disclosure agreement states, I will let you know what you can and cannot print. You can print this: nudity and sexuality are mutually exclusive. Although, we are all nude, this isn't about sex. It's about freedom from the textile world."

Bill smirked. "That's way too boring to print and it has

nothing to do with the story I'm writing. Besides all that, I think it's all bullshit. You people are exhibitionists. You get off on being naked in front of other people. Why try to moralize it?"

"There is nothing wrong with what we are doing. Humans are the only animals that wear clothing. It isn't natural. About 70,000 years ago, humans started migrating to the northern, more frigid regions of the world, and discovered they could handle the cold by covering themselves with the skins of the animals they killed to eat. At some point, mythology made it wrong to go uncovered, according to certain tribes. Clothing should always be a matter of pragmatics, and not about modesty."

"I'm sitting here nude talking to you. If I thought it was wrong, I wouldn't be here. However, although I've managed to avoid arousal, I do find this titillating. Madison seems well adjusted, but she is a beautiful girl with a knockout body. You are worried about perverts and have every right to be. She looks old enough, but we both know she's not. Do you really think she should be exposed like this?"

Jeremy nodded. "Do you think she would be less attractive with clothes on? We do have some pervs here and they have tried things. I don't think Madison has been molested, but I'm pretty sure she's not a virgin either. Still, that's a concern of the textile world, too. If not more so," he said.

"And it's none of my business. I think you have a right to raise your daughter as you please. I like Madison. She's smart and charming, and I think she can take care of herself. You've done a good job."

"Do you have children, Mr. Clark?"

"No. My wife and I were very political in the seventies and we believed that it was selfish to bring a child into this screwed-up world. We changed our minds, but my wife had surgery to avoid ovarian cancer. So, we haven't been able to have children. We thought about adoption, but we decided that we

OTHA FOSTER

really weren't the parenting types."

"Madison was an accident, but she's been the best accident I've ever had. It was definitely selfish. But you're right; she can take care of herself."

"Well, none of that is why I'm here," Bill said, "I just want to know about Teresa Rosales, although I am now curious about Chuck's partner."

"Let me dispense with Chuck's situation first. My father was admittedly a homophobe, but he wouldn't have killed anyone. I agree with Chuck that Frankie's death did sound like an Aztec sacrifice, but the cult that was here before didn't practice that. They were just a handful of peaceful Mexicans that were trying to go back to the beliefs of their forefathers before the Spanish came and forced their religion on them. My father pretended to be one of them when he started, but he pretty much took the place over. One by one, an Anglo family replaced each Mexican family. My father accomplished this by calling immigration on anyone who tried to oppose him. And that leads to Teresa Rosales. As far as I know, Teresa was picked up with her family after her father tried to lead a revolt against my father."

"Did you see immigration take her away?" Bill asked.

"No. They--the Border Patrol--always came in the middle of the night. I was asleep when they came, but I would hear about it the next day."

"So, could it be possible that Teresa escaped."

Jeremy nodded. "I suppose, but it seems unlikely trained law enforcement officers would let a naked 14-year-old girl get past them."

Bill nodded. He thought that was probably true. "Could she have been at a friend's house? You know—a sleepover?" he asked

"She could have been, but that wouldn't explain why

she would have collapsed naked on your front porch. This wasn't nudist place back then."

Bill was finding more questions than answers, so he decided to change directions. "You knew her well?" he asked.

"I was three years older than Teresa, so I didn't hang out with her much. Young Whitman sniffed around her. I kept telling him that she was jailbait, but that didn't dissuade him. He was nineteen at the time. Of course, since Teresa was an 'illegal' he knew he could probably get away with it." Jeremy said, and then paused and stared off into space for a second.

"Do you think he had sex with her?" Bill asked.

Jeremy's eyes glistened a little. "I don't know if he did, but I know he wanted to. And Larry had always been good about getting what he wanted," he said

"If I write a story, what am I allowed to write?"

"That Teresa Rosales was here and, as far as Fifth Sun management knows, she was taken back to Mexico. That is a fact, but if you find out anything else about Teresa you can write what you want, because she was not a member of the resort. Her past is not protected by the non-disclosure agreement. That goes for anything you find out about my father and his days as leader of the cult that took over the place from the Aztec cult. My father was a sorry bastard. You can write whatever you want."

"Chuck said your father was gay."

Jeremy laughed, and said, "I wouldn't be a bit surprised, but he really hated Chuck. I'd be surprised if he had a fling with Chuck."

"He said your father had an affair with Frankie."

Jeremy nodded. "Chuck told me that. I didn't believe it at the time but looking back I can almost believe that. My father was really upset when Frankie died."

Not having a notepad or recorder made it difficult for

Bill to conduct a good interview. He would often write down questions while people were answering another question, and it helped him keep on track. He was at a loss now. "I guess that's about it," he said. "I can't think of anything else to ask. Just one more thing, though. Do you know if there is anyone left around here from the original Aztec cult?"

Jeremy shook his head. "I'm sure they are all dead or somewhere in Mexico," he said. "The only thing left are the stones they used for worship. They are down near the lake. It's a popular place for late night parties. A few couples find it fun to have sex on the altar."

"There is an altar?"

"Oh sure, but like I said, I don't think they ever sacrificed anyone on it." He pointed over Bill's left shoulder. "If you follow that trail it will lead you to it. There's a sign hanging from a tree before you get there. On one side it says 'c'mon down' and the other 'private party.' If it says 'private party' it means you can still go down if you want, but be prepared for more than nudity. You should go check it out."

If Jeremy had any other information for Bill, Bill couldn't think what it would be. Anyway, Jeremy stood up, which Bill took as the end of the interview.

"I certainly will," Bill said, "but for now I think I'll go watch the softball game."

The softball game was being played in the middle of a grassy field. The spectators were sitting on blankets on a gentle slope. There was no backstop, lime baselines, or pitcher's mound. The bases looked homemade. Cathy was sitting on a large blanket with Whitman. She waved Bill over. Reluctantly, he walked over and sat down next to her.

At this point, Bill had adjusted to the nudity. It really wasn't that different than going to the beach. It's sort of amazing how much importance people put on a few inches of fabric. When Bill thought about it, the fabric tended to guide one's eyes to the area that was covered. With everyone nude, Bill found himself less drawn to the breasts and genital areas. Actually, he started imagining what people looked like with clothes on. The game started and when the people started swinging, throwing, and running, Bill, once again, became painfully aware of the nudity.

Bill turned to Cathy and said, "I think the sports world would completely change if all athletes were required to play nude."

Cathy laughed. "I would become a sports fan, for sure."

"I think everything would be better naked," Whitman said.

For a few moments they sat in silence, and then Cathy said, "I'm going to go find some beer." She was gone in a shot and it left Bill alone on the blanket with the one person he despised most in the world.

"I saw you talking to Jeremy, earlier," Whitman said. "Did he shed any light?"

"He mentioned that you might have taken advantage of Teresa Rosales when she was fourteen," Bill said, bluntly.

The politician's head spun around, and he glared at Bill. "That was a long time ago and totally not true," he said, "If anyone had a fling with her it was Jeremy."

Bill could usually tell if someone was lying. Still, Whitman was a politician. He was a professional liar. "Well, I suppose I can clear it up by finding Teresa Rosales and asking her. I don't know what the statute of limitations is for statutory rape, but I do know there are no limitations in the court of public opinion--especially for a politician trying to get re-elected. That information is also not guarded by any non-disclosure agreement."

Whitman laughed and said, "It could still be libel. I've been playing this game a long time now, Bill. It would be a serious error in judgment to try and beat me at my own game here in my own state. I'm a lot more skillful than those hillbillies in southwest New Mexico. Do you really think you know where Teresa Rosales is?"

Bill didn't answer.

Whitman smiled. "I didn't think so," he said. "Still, it would be nice to see her again. I'd be curious what she would have to say. Be sure and let me know if you do really find her."

"No offense, Senator," Bill said, "but you'd be the last person I'd talk to if I found her."

"None taken. If anything, I'm flattered. Glad to know I'm still under your skin."

"Don't be," Bill said. "You aren't that important to anyone." Bill got up and walked away. He met Cathy walking towards him toting a small bucket filled with ice and Coronas.

"Where are you going?" Cathy asked. "I got us some beer."

"I'm sorry, but I don't like the company you keep. Are you sure you know what you are doing with that guy?"

She had been smiling, but the smile faded. "No," she said, softly, "but it is something I have to do."

Bill didn't know what she was talking about, but he was fairly certain it was none of his business, and he could tell it was pretty serious. "Just be careful," he said.

"I really appreciate your concern," she said, "but I have to do this."

She walked back to Whitman.

CHAPTER 20

Bill went looking for Charlotte. He wanted to get his clothes on and go back to the motel, even though he didn't think Charlotte would be too keen on the idea. Still, it was worth a shot.

When he found her, she told him to go get the key to her bungalow out of her locker. "They won't let us out of the gate now," she said.

"Why not?"

"The store is closed, and you'll have a hard time convincing someone here to get dressed to let us out."

"So, we are basically naked prisoners here."

She didn't answer, but her face told Bill that what he was saying was basically true, and it troubled her, as well.

Bill said, "It's funny to me that all you people are totally exposed on the outside, but all seem to be hiding something."

Charlotte smirked. "There is a difference in being nude and naked. Naked means you are vulnerable, but nude simply means having no clothes on."

"I don't suppose if I asked you to tell me what you are hiding you would tell me?"

She shook her head. "Everyone has secrets. Exposing one's secrets makes one vulnerable. Besides if you were a better reporter, you would've already figured out mine."

That genuinely stung. "I don't suppose it's any of my business, anyway," Bill said.

"I didn't say that," she said, "but there are times when giving people too much information can be dangerous. At this point, it is like the movie line, 'you can't handle the truth.'"

She turned and walked away. A tingle went up and down Bill's spine, but he didn't know why. All he knew was that he had to stay here, anyway, so he thought he should continue to look around for the secrets this place held.

While Bill was walking back to the locker room, out of the corner of his eye he noticed a familiar looking pick-up sitting in the parking lot. Adrenaline coursed through his veins as he realized it was Cathy's ex-husband's truck. Bill didn't think that guy was the nudist type, but someone must've let him in. Bill hadn't seen him, but it's harder to distinguish people in a sea of naked bodies. Bill just hoped the man wasn't up on a hill watching Bill through the scope of a deer rifle. Maybe he was watching Whitman.

Bill rushed into the dressing room and sat down. He was trying to think of what he should do. He decided to get dressed so he wouldn't feel so vulnerable, but he knew his clothes wouldn't protect him from a bullet. Also, walking around dressed in a nudist resort would just make him easier to spot.

Bill walked out of the dressing room and went to the office. The door was locked, and no one answered when he knocked. He returned to the dressing room and found the key to Charlotte's bungalow. He found her bungalow rather easily. He unlocked the door and went inside. He pulled closed the shade on the one window and lay down on one of the beds. As his heart rate began to slow down, he began to feel a little sleepy. Soon he was sound asleep. When he awoke it was dark.

After the long nap, Bill decided that he was probably being a little paranoid about Jerry Elkins. Lots of people in Texas drove Silverado pick-ups, and Bill reasoned that if Jerry wanted him dead, he'd already be dead.

Bill looked out of the window of the bungalow. There was a bonfire going near the spot where they had played softball. Bill imagined that was where the party was. He wasn't in a partying mood, but he was curious to see what Cathy was up to. Reluctantly, he shed his clothes and took them back to the locker room.

Just as Bill reached the bonfire, he saw Cathy and Whitman walking away down a trail. He held back a little but followed. It soon occurred to him that they were probably headed down to the altar that Jeremy had told him about. He suspected that he knew why they would be going, and still felt an urge to follow. Bill knew what he was feeling was jealousy, even though he knew he had no right to feel that way. Still, he followed. He was encouraged when they arrived at the "c'mon down" sign and didn't switch it to "private party." Of course, it would have been too dark to see anyway.

They arrived at the altar, which was illuminated by torches. Bill found a spot behind a bush to hide. In the torchlight Bill could see another person, a female, standing by the altar, but in the shadow. Her face was too dark for him to see. Whitman and Cathy stepped up to the altar, and the woman moved forward to greet them. As she stepped into the light, Bill realized it was Madison.

Without preamble, Whitman took Madison's hand and led her to the altar. He motioned for her to lie down on it. Bill's mind raced. Surely, they weren't going sacrifice her. Cathy seemed to be in a trance, watching the scene with dead eyes. Whitman walked around the altar and seemed to be posing Madison like he would a corpse. He pulled her arms out and down to the side, the stepped to her feet. He grabbed her ankles and separated her legs wide, and then he bent her legs as if preparing her for a gynecological exam. It became clear what Whitman was going to do. Bill stepped out from his hiding place and said, "Don't even think about it."

Whitman smiled and said, "Clark, I'm really glad you are here. I was afraid you wouldn't show up."

That confused Bill. "Why did you think I would?" he asked.

"It was part of the plan," Cathy said.

"Whatever," Bill said, feeling the anger beginning to boil, "but any plans of you touching that girl aren't going to happen. You were about to commit a felony. One that releases me from the disclosure agreement, and from kicking your sorry ass!"

Whitman laughed. "I'm not going to have sex with this girl," he said, "You are—or at least it's going to appear that you are."

"We'll see about that," Bill said and started walking towards the altar. It was too late to look around, but Bill saw Cathy's eyes widen in surprise. Before he could turn, he felt a pinch in his back and then all his muscles convulsed. He fell helplessly to the ground, convulsing. Bill couldn't control any of his muscles, but he could see Whitman step towards him. Whitman and another man Bill couldn't see picked him up by the armpits and drug him towards the altar. They wrapped Bill's arms from the front around a large wooden post and cuffed his hands. They let Bill go and he fell to his knees leaning against the post.

Slowly, Bill's muscle control returned, and he could stand. He looked around and saw only Whitman, Cathy, and Madison. "What are you going to do to me?" he asked.

Whitman said, "A couple of things, but ultimately I am going to kill you."

Cathy and Madison's eyes widened with fear. Apparently, this was part of the plan Whitman had not shared.

"And how do you plan to do that?" Bill asked.

"At sunrise, I am going to sacrifice you to the Sun God."

"Like you did to Frankie?"

Whitman's eyebrows shot up. "You know about Frankie! Wow, you are a good reporter. Do you know why?" he asked.

"I imagine Frankie had some information on you that would have affected your re-election," Bill said. "Isn't that all you ever care about, Whitman? Also, I imagine you actually believe that a human sacrifice will help stop droughts."

Whitman nodded and said, "I am impressed, Bill. How did you figure that out?"

"I didn't. Sheriff Prine did. I imagine he also figured out that you had raped Teresa Rosales. Why did you kill him the way you did? Why didn't you sacrifice him?"

"I didn't need to," Whitman said, shrugging. "There was no drought."

"What about Cathy's father?"

Cathy's face didn't flinch, but Whitman glanced around to look at her. "I didn't kill your father, Cathy. I promise I didn't," he said.

"I know," she said. "He killed himself."

Something was wrong here. Had he convinced her that her father really had killed himself? Was this bastard that good? "How do you expect to explain my disappearance? Or are you going to dump my body in the Frio and let them fish me out?" Bill asked.

"You're going on the lam, Bill," he said. "By this time tomorrow you will have a warrant out for your arrest. Your hot wife will hear about how you had sex with young Madison here and got caught. Everyone will be looking for you everywhere, except for the pit I'll be throwing your body in after the sacrifice.

Bill looked at Cathy and Madison. "Why are you going

along with this?" he asked.

"Larry is a powerful man," Cathy said. "I'm tired of losers. He promises a great future. With your sacrifice, Larry will become as powerful as a king. Madison and I will be his queens."

"You will be his concubines," Bill said. "His whores."

They both just smiled. "Enough of this," Whitman said. "Madison, please do what I asked you to do."

Madison walked over to Bill and pushed herself between Bill and the post. She pressed her body tightly against Bill's and wrapped her arms around him. She went up on her toes and attempted to kiss him. Bill turned his head to avoid her kiss, but as her lips grazed his cheek, he realized she had something in her mouth. Realizing what it was he stopped and kissed her back with lingering open-mouthed kiss. A flash of bright light distracted Bill slightly, but he continued to kiss until the exchange was made. Cathy had taken their picture.

As their lips parted, Bill looked Madison in the eyes and saw what he had already surmised. She was not a part of this. Not voluntarily.

"See you at sunrise, Bill," Whitman said.

Bill didn't respond.

Whitman put out all the torches and it went completely black. All Bill could see was the glow from the bonfire up the hill which was now just glowing ashes. He wanted to get out of the cuffs and beat the hell out of Whitman, but somewhere in the woods there was a person with a stun gun. He stood perfectly still listening for any sound.

After a long time of listening, Bill determined that he was actually alone. He leaned against the pole and was able to get his hands to his mouth and pull out the key that Madison had passed to him when they kissed. Bill undid the cuffs and cautiously started up the path. He froze when he got to the top and saw a silhouette against the glowing coals of the bonfire.

"It's me," Madison said.

"I was coming to help you," Bill said.

"I knew you would, but I don't need help. I can handle Whitman. You need to get away from here."

"Okay, let me go get my clothes."

"You can't go back. You have to get away from here."

"How?"

She pointed up into the sky. "You see that star? Follow it through the woods. You'll find a gap in the fence. Keep going north until you find a house."

"If I show up naked at some person's house in the middle of the night I'll get shot."

"There's only one house you are going to find and it's your old house. No one lives there, but that's where you'll find a place to hide."

"I'd really rather not do this naked."

"It's either naked or dead."

Bill nodded, turned and ran. If it was this distressing for Bill at this age, how much more must it have been for Teresa at fourteen? Bill lost count of how many times he tripped and fell as he ran to the woods. His feet felt as if they were being put through a meat grinder.

Occasionally, Bill would stop and listen to hear if anyone were following. There was no sound, so he kept running. When he came to the fence, he didn't see the gap. He looked up at the star and realized he had gone a little off course. He went left along the fence line. Eventually, Bill found the gap. It wasn't a big one, but he managed to squeeze through, but not without adding more scratches to the ones he'd already acquired.

He continued running, and though he knew he had only

been running for no more than a few minutes it seemed as if it had been hours. Bill was completely exhausted and now he was staggering. Soon he discovered the highway and limped down it towards the direction that was now familiar. There were no cars in sight. Soon he came upon the dirt road that led to his childhood home. He followed it. Delirious with relief he found the house and crawled up onto the porch. He didn't really pass out, but he was so exhausted he lay down very near where Teresa had years ago, carefully feeling for the broken glass. The glass from the broken window was gone. Someone had swept the porch. He was almost asleep when a light was in his face and a woman's voice said, "You can't stay here. Come inside."

Bill looked past the light and could make out an outline of a face. It was a familiar face--one from many years ago. "Who are you?" Bill asked.

"I'm Teresa Rosales," she said. "You need to get inside. People will be looking for you."

CHAPTER 21

Teresa helped Bill to his feet, and she opened the door to the house and guided him inside. On the floor where Bill's family couch used to be, were some blankets and a Coleman lantern. Teresa picked up a blanket and draped it over Bill's bare shoulders. "Have a seat on that blanket," she said.

Bill did as she said, and he looked up to see her. She was older, much older, but he recognized the face he'd seen all those years ago. "What are you doing here?" he asked. "How did you know I'd be here?"

She sat down cross-legged on the floor across from Bill. "You really don't know?" she asked

"I don't know, but I have an idea that your son had something to do with it."

She smiled and then Ricky stepped into the room out of the shadows. "It didn't take much detective work, I'm sure," Ricky said, "but how did you know you were looking for my mother?"

Bill laughed and said, "You're right. I'm no detective, but I've been around Mexican people all my life and I know about their custom of giving their children the mother's maiden name as a middle name. I saw it on your degree in your office."

Teresa reached into an ice chest and pulled out a bottle of water. She handed it to Bill, and he twisted off the lid and gulped it down. He drank it a little too fast and he was afraid he would toss it back up, but thankfully the feeling faded.

"Why did you wait so long to bring it up?" Ricky asked, leaning against the wall. Bill imagined it was hard to sit on the floor when one has all that police equipment on. "You probably could've avoided all this."

"I didn't know who I could trust. I still don't. I find it a little strange that you guys are here. How did you know I was coming here? Did Madison call you?"

"No, Cathy did," Ricky said.

Adrenaline shot through Bill's veins. "She's sleeping with Whitman and he's the one trying to kill me," he said.

"Yes," Teresa said, "but she's also the one who gave Madison the handcuff key to give to you. She's on your side."

"That would be a relief if it was true. She took pictures of me kissing Madison. It would be nice if those got destroyed."

Ricky shook his head. "No, they are already in the hands of a writer for the *Texas Monthly*. The *Austin Statesman* has already written the story. Tomorrow you will be believed to be a child molester and a fugitive from justice. A warrant has already been issued for your arrest."

Bill sighed. "It doesn't sound like Cathy is on my side much," he said. "Larry Whitman is the molester and I believe he's also a murderer."

A tear trickled down Teresa's cheek. "Cathy's doing what she has to, and as for Whitman being a molester, I know that. He molested me forty years ago. He was raping me while immigration came and got my parents. They would have caught me if I hadn't escaped and came here."

It was then that Bill realized he now had the opportunity to find out the answers to the questions he had come here to ask. "Please tell me what happened," he pleaded. "I've always wondered. Let's just forget the rest for now."

"Where do you want me to start?"

"From as early as you can remember—the beginning."

She nodded. "My family was nearly starving in Mexico. I was only two when we came across the border for my father to find work."

"So, you were not born here?" Bill asked.

"No, I am a citizen now, but I was undocumented back then. It was easier to get here in those days; we didn't have to pay a coyote to get here. My father got a job with Milton Forester, the man that this town was named for. He owned all this land and he raised sheep. Mr. Forester built houses on the land where Fifth Sun is now. He was a very generous man. He provided my family with a place to live and paid my father better than he had to. He even paid all our medical bills and built the school to give all of us children an education. He knew we were in the country illegally, but he treated us like we had a right to be here.

"When Mr. Forester died, he willed the land we lived on to the Mexican families that lived there. He didn't have any surviving family so no one contested it. But since none of us were legal, we couldn't really own the property. It was my father's idea to incorporate as a church. We were able to get the teachers at the school to be a board of trustees. They couldn't do anything with the property without approval of the membership from the church. We could not be legal citizens of the United States, but we could be members of a church."

"That was pretty clever of your father," Bill said. "No one ever challenged it?"

"Not really," she said. "All of the local ranchers depended on migrant workers, both legal and illegal, so they didn't put up a fuss. Father Gomez brought up the issue about our doctrines once, and that stirred up some controversy. My father despised the Roman Catholic Church. He thought it was totally corrupt. When he started getting questioned about the church's beliefs, he began studying the Aztecs and professed those as our beliefs. My father thought all religion was superstitious and silly, but he was willing to pretend to keep the auditors away."

Bill nodded and said, "And it worked until Jeremiah showed up."

She frowned. "He seemed like a nice man at first. He promised us that he could help us get citizenships without the regular red tape. He said all we needed was to make our church a little more mainstream.

"From the beginning, my father thought he was a snake oil salesman, but the others liked him. He didn't seem to be dangerous, and I don't guess he really was. Jeremiah Porter was full of crap, but it was the Whitmans that were the truly evil ones. Larry's father was the one calling immigration on people when they disagreed with Jeremiah's prophecies. Jeremiah really wanted to increase the church and he didn't want anyone to leave. Alfred Whitman was obviously planning on stealing everything away from the people of the church. And he did it slowly--one family at a time.

"When my father found out what was happening, he went and told Jeremiah. Jeremiah was outraged, but that was when the sheriff found the body from the first sacrifice. We didn't do sacrifices, but since we emulated the Aztecs who did do human sacrifices, the suspicion fell on us. I'm pretty sure it was old man Whitman that did the sacrifice and threatened Jeremiah with exposure to the press if Jeremiah crossed him."

"What kept Whitman from taking over?" Bill asked.

"When Larry Whitman started raping and killing the young Mexican girls, that put a kink in his father's plan. My father declared war, but Whitman was white and had the power of law on his side. There was no way for my father to win. The lights from the Border Patrol interrupted Larry's raping me or I wouldn't have escaped. When Larry got off of me to see what was going on, I kicked him in the nuts and took off running. I didn't stop until I got here on your porch.

"When your mother revived me, and I ran away and hid. I was still hiding in the woods as I watched as she reported everything to the sheriff's deputies. I was cold, tired, hungry and afraid. I had no idea what I was going to do. I don't know how she knew I was there, but your mother came back out on the porch. She brought out a plate of food and sat it on the edge. I don't really know what she said, because I didn't speak English, but her words sounded kind. I really had no other choice. I walked out and got the food. She wrapped a blanket around me, and I slept on your couch. I hid in a closet while your mother got you ready for school. When she came back from taking you to school, she brought Father Gomez back with her. He convinced me to come to the church. He helped me find my mother in Mexico."

"What happened to your father?" Bill asked.

Tears flowed down her cheeks. "My father escaped the Border Patrol, and he went back and killed Alfred Whitman with his bare hands. He was arrested, sentenced, and eventually executed for murder. My mother died soon after."

"He didn't know about Larry raping you?"

"No, he thought it was the old man that was killing the girls. He died thinking he'd killed my murderer, not knowing that it was Alfred's son who'd committed the murders and rapes."

Bill shook his head in disgust.

Teresa continued. "For years I have tried to think of ways to get revenge on Whitman for what he did to my family and me, but he's too powerful. We gave up. When Ricky and I heard that you were here to do a story our first thought was that you would dig up the truth and put us all in danger. We hoped you might be able to expose Whitman, but deep down we knew something like this would happen."

Ricky nodded and said, "I tried to warn you when you got here. You should have left when you had the chance."

Bill nodded and then said, "One more thing. Can you tell me what happened to my mother?"

Teresa smiled. "I can, but I won't," she said. "Not now. It isn't my place."

"Whose place, is it?"

"You are clever. You'll figure it out. I'm surprised you haven't already."

Bill saw the determination in her expression. She wasn't going to tell him anything. He turned and looked at Ricky. "Are you going to arrest me?"

"I will if you want me to," Ricky said. "Whitman will send the Texas Rangers. Most of them are decent guys, but I'm sure he has some of them in his pocket. They also have a reputation for not following the rules."

"Cathy told me to trust her. She has an agenda. I don't know what it is, but maybe I should see what she is up to."

Ricky laughed. "Cathy isn't trustworthy, but she might be your only hope. She asked me not to let you contact her or you'd blow her cover. You're going to have to figure out your part in her plan yourself."

Bill looked around at the old house. It made him sad to be there. He missed his parents and this place made him think of them. "Can you take me to your jail for the night? I'd like to call my wife, and then get a good night's sleep. Maybe what I need to do will be clear to me in the morning."

Ricky took Bill to his motel to get his clothes, and then took him to the jail. He let Bill take a shower. When Bill finished, Ricky showed him to his office. He handed Bill the phone. Valerie answered on the second ring. She didn't say hello, but simply said, "They faxed me the pictures."

"It isn't how it looks." Bill said and explained what happened.

"It pretty clearly shows you kissing a naked teenage girl, and it looks like you are enjoying it. I'm an open-minded woman, but what am I supposed to think?"

Bill understood. "I explained what happened. What else can I say?"

"I don't know, Bill. I just don't know."

Bill hung up the phone wishing the call had gone differently. He was convinced that he hadn't done anything wrong, but he knew those images would always haunt Valerie. Everyone that saw them would think he was guilty.

"I'm not booking you," Ricky said, softly. "If someone shows up, I shut the door to the cell. If you want to leave and head back to New Mexico, I won't stop you."

Bill shook his head. "That would only make things worse," he said. "I'll just try and get some sleep. I think I know what I'm going to do."

"And what is that?"

"I think I want you to turn me over to the Rangers."

Ricky's eyes widened. "That could be suicide," he said.

"Maybe, but it will be the last thing Whitman expects. If I do what he expects, he'll win. There might be a chance if I do something he doesn't expect."

CHAPTER 22

When Bill woke up, Ricky brought him some coffee and a copy of the Austin Statesman. There weren't any pictures, but he'd made the front page. The headline read: "Rangers Search for Nudist Journalist Child Molester."

Bill didn't read the story. He didn't need to. He'd already written the story in his head as he would have written it. He did think he would have had a better headline.

"Did Cathy do a story for the Gazette?" Bill asked.

"Her office is closed, but the paper doesn't come out until next Tuesday. She'll probably just print the AP story."

"That's a shame," Bill smirked. "She's got all the inside dope."

"Do you still want me to call the Texas Rangers?"

"Yeah, I do."

"Do you want me find you a good attorney? I know a few."

Bill shook his head. "I don't want an attorney."

"That's madness, Bill," Ricky said. "You're innocent. A good attorney can get you off."

"If I lawyer up right away it will leave everything to people's imagination. An attorney will keep me out of jail, but his strategy will be to delay. I'm going to confess."

"That's just crazy."

"Probably, but the insane route is the only one that

hasn't been attempted. Maybe craziness is the only way to go."

Ricky shook his head. "I don't get it, but it's your neck. Where do you want to meet them?" he asked.

"Can they come get me at the Blue Bonnet? I'd really like some of the Bonnet's biscuits and gravy while we wait."

When they walked into the Blue Bonnet it was clear from their expressions that everyone in there had read the Statesman. For a brief minute he was afraid that these soft-spoken ranchers might just take a rope and lynch him.

"Why isn't he in cuffs, Sheriff?" one cowboy asked.

"Cause he ain't under arrest, yet, Emmett," Ricky replied. "Why don't you just let me do my job as I see fit."

No one else said a word. Sally took Bill's order, but she was looking at him in disgust. When she brought him his breakfast she said, "I thought you were a loyal married man, but I guess I just wasn't young enough for you."

"I'm sorry if I hurt you, Sally," Bill said. The tears in her eyes were angry tears. She wasn't hurt, just pissed.

Bill, as it turned out, didn't have much of an appetite and he was glad to see the Texas Ranger when he arrived. He introduced himself as Ben Minsky and took a seat. "Mr. Clark, I've not spoken to the victim, yet. Her father seems to think you're being set up. He wouldn't let me talk to his daughter without an attorney."

"Did you speak to any of the other witnesses?"

"What other witnesses?"

Bill smiled and asked, "Mr. Minsky, who do you think took those pictures?"

He frowned and said, "I hadn't thought about it. I see what you mean. Do you know who took the pictures?"

Bill nodded.

"Are you going to tell me?"

"Not now. Not here. I'll tell you what. I'm going to confess to the whole thing and make your job easy, but I want to do it in public. I want to confess in front of the press."

"That's not the way we do things."

"I hear the Texas Rangers don't always let the rules dictate. Is that not true?"

His face turned purple. "We just want to get the criminals off the streets. If we have to bend the rules a little, we do!"

Bill smiled again. This was going to be easier than he thought. "I'm asking you to bend. You can be a hero and bring in a child molester and have him confess to the world, or I can get an attorney and fight it all in court."

Minsky took the bait.

Ricky took Bill back to the cell and Minsky went to work on the press conference. Bill was afraid the ranger might call some superiors who would shut this down before it got started, but he got on the phone and started calling reporters. Bill expected him to call a few newspapers, but when Ricky brought Bill his lunch, he told him that Minsky had even called some network television reporters.

"Do you think they'll come?"

Ricky nodded. "I've never heard of someone confessing during a press conference before, but I'm sure they'll come. This guy is probably going to lose his job. He'll get his fifteen minutes of fame, though."

Bill laughed and said, "Well, you sure knew how to pick the right man for the job."

146

"Do you think this will work? I think I know what you plan to do, but if you don't handle it correctly. It'll backfire."

"I don't think I really have anything to lose."

By three that afternoon, Faytonville was a three-ring circus. Bill looked out at the sea of news vehicles with satellite equipment. All of them were here to capture a man's self-destruction on live television. What had this world come to?

Ranger Minsky walked up to the bars of Bill's cell. Ricky unlocked it. "It's showtime," Minsky said.

They fitted Bill with a bulletproof vest and put him in cuffs, a belly chain and shackles. They helped him shuffle to the door of the courthouse. "Wait here," Minsky said, and then he walked outside. He was greeted with loud applause.

"What a bunch of stupid sheep," Ricky murmured.

Minsky made an awkward statement and moved aside as Ricky escorted Bill to the microphones. It became deathly silent as Bill made a show of unfolding a piece of paper, even though he had nothing written on it. He had rehearsed what he would say many times in his head.

"A few years ago, a prominent member of the Texas Legislature told me he was a member of a nudist resort in south Texas. He told me that he would help me get in if I wanted to come. During our conversation I confessed to him that I liked really young girls. He told me that if I came to Fifth Sun resort, I would be able to have as many young girls as I wanted, at any age. I found a way to pretend I was doing a story and came here. I confess that I hooked up with a seventeen-year-old girl. I kissed her and she pressed her nude body up against me. I was about to have sex with her when someone snapped our picture. Fearing consequences, I ran away."

Minsky, oblivious to the can of worms Bill had just opened, stepped up to the microphones and said, "You may ask

Mr. Clark a few questions, but then I will be booking him for attempted aggravated sexual assault."

A reporter stood and asked, "The obvious question I want to ask is who the hell was the prominent member of the legislature."

"I promised to keep that confidential."

Another reporter jumped up. "But you're suggesting that this man might be a child molester, too. Aren't you covering for someone that is as guilty as you?"

"I have no doubt that he likes young girls, but I'm not going to disclose his identity."

Bill didn't see who asked the next question, but he heard it. "Who took the pictures?"

Bill leaned into the microphone. "It was Cathy Elkins, publisher, editor, and reporter for the Faytonville Gazette."

That was enough. Bill didn't need to do anything else.

Ricky escorted Bill back to the cell as Minsky continued fielding questions from the press. As Ricky undid the restraints he said, "I don't understand. Why didn't you just tell them about Whitman? You didn't have a problem throwing Cathy under the bus."

"I'm giving him a little rope to hang himself," Bill said. "He can't deny an accusation that hasn't been made, yet. He'll think he still has a chance to cover it up."

"Then why did you give them Cathy's name?"

"To force her hand. She got me into this mess. I still think she's on Whitman's side."

Ricky shook his head. "I know I warned you not to trust her, but you're wrong about this," he said.

"Then I'm probably screwed. But there are a lot of unanswered questions, and I think only Cathy has the answers.

Let me ask you one. Is it possible that Cathy's father actually did commit suicide?"

Ricky shrugged and said, "That's what the coroner ruled it. He was depressed at the time. He and Cathy hadn't spoken in years."

"Was that when you and Cathy hooked up? When she came to ask you to investigate her father's death?"

Ricky shook his head. "She never asked me to investigate her father's death. She just wanted me to look for her daughter."

"What?"

"Yeah. She didn't tell you?" Ricky asked, with the surprised expression.

"No. What happened to her daughter?"

"As I understand it, she was kidnapped as a baby from the hospital. We hunted for her for years but found nothing. That was about seventeen years ago. Cathy believes it was someone from the Aztec cult that took her. I didn't have any probable cause to search the place. Cathy joined the resort, believing she would find her daughter, or at least what had happened to her."

"I think she might have found her," Bill said. "She may not know it, yet, but I think she may believe her daughter was another one of Whitman's victims."

"Do you think she's going to kill Whitman?"

"If she wanted to kill him, she would have done so already," Bill said. "She may still kill him eventually, but she wants to ruin him first."

"Well, that makes things better for you, doesn't it?"

"Maybe," Bill said, shaking his head. "I'm just a disposable pawn. I no longer matter. But maybe she'll be able to help."

Minsky talked to the press for over an hour. Finally, he entered Bill's cell and asked for the paper Bill had used. "I need that confession signed," he said. "It'll do until I get it typed up."

Bill handed him the blank paper.

"What the hell--"

"I didn't say anything about signing a confession. I just told you I'd confess for the press."

"But that is worthless if you don't sign a written confession."

Bill laughed and said, "It's all worthless anyway. You never read me my rights. Everything I said out there was bullshit —well, almost all of it. I did kiss that girl, but it was all a set-up. I was handcuffed at the time and Madison slipped me the key to the handcuffs by kissing me. The senator was going to kill me, and she saved my life. I didn't have sex with her and never intended to."

Minsky turned more shades of red and purple than Bill thought possible. "You know you probably just cost me my job," he said

"I'm sorry about that, but that's probably a good thing, because you aren't very good at it. However, you might be able to salvage it by getting off your ass and going out to Fifth Sun. You need to question Cathy Elkins and Madison Porter. You might even find Jeremy Porter willing to talk, since his livelihood may be in jeopardy."

Minsky was pissed, but he nodded in agreement. He wasn't getting anything accomplished sitting around the courthouse. His dreams of fame and fortune just got dashed. Now all he could do is try to wipe some of the egg off his face. He turned to leave.

"Minsky," Bill said, "You might want to go find Jerry Elkins, as well. I think he played a big role in this."

CHAPTER 23

Ricky went and picked up some burgers from Dairy Queen for his and Bill's dinner, and they sat around his desk and ate.

"You know you still haven't been booked, yet," Ricky said. "Until you are, you could still walk around free. You could walk out and get in your rental car and go home. Since Minsky took over the case, it would be no skin off my nose."

"I don't want to add absconding to whatever charges I'm going to be charged with," Bill said. "I figure that even if I don't get nailed for the aggravated sexual assault, I'll at least get charged with obstruction. All of the Texas Rangers can't be idiots."

Ricky shrugged. "I feel bad about screwing a fellow law officer," he said, "but the Texas Rangers have never been particularly popular among Mexican people. They could have sought justice for my mother all those years ago, but they wrote her off like everyone else still does. As I see it, the only Anglo that ever cared about my mother was your mother. I will help you any way I can in gratitude to her."

"That's good news," Bill said. "I think I found the one person I can trust. I've been played like a fiddle by everyone else in this town since I got here."

Ricky had a television in his office. They watched the news reports on every channel they could. It appeared that either no one had yet discovered who the mysterious legislator was, or they were just not reporting it. Bill guessed it was probably the latter.

Bill's pictures were splashed all over the news. Madison's face and breasts were blurred. At this point, Bill figured he was one of the most despised people in Texas. Ricky's phone rang. He answered it. "Yes ma'am. He's right here," Ricky said, and handed Bill the phone.

"I haven't any more comments for the press," Bill said into the receiver.

"Not even for the Copper City Daily Press?" Valerie asked.

"After our last conversation, I feel that your paper might do me the most damage."

Valerie sighed and said, "I've been watching the news. It looks like you have yourself in a hell of a mess."

"Yeah, and I'm afraid I may need an attorney at some point. I'd try to get them to let me have a public defender, but I think the judge is going to decide we have too many assets to get free legal help."

"Any chance of the charges being dropped?" she asked

"I haven't actually been charged with anything yet, but I just pissed off the Texas Ranger on the case. He'll be going for castration. I imagine I'll be charged with something."

"Well, believe it or not, most of your friends back here believe you are not guilty. Actually, they said they thought you were innocent, but I corrected them on that."

"Good for you," Bill said, wincing a little.

"They started a defense fund. It's almost enough for a retainer, I think. Do you want me to call someone?"

"No, I don't need one, yet, "he replied. "Cathy might still come through for me."

There was a long pause. "Okay, I believe you didn't have

sex with the girl, but what about Cathy?" Valerie asked. I noted the quiver in her voice.

"You may find this hard to believe," Bill said, "but I actually haven't had sex with anyone, despite the fact I've had offers from a reporter, waitress, and a county clerk."

There was another long pause. Finally, she said, "You hadn't mentioned the county clerk. What's her name?"

"Chuck."

She chuckled and said, "Okay, I want to hear about that later, but I still have a paper to put out."

Valerie hung up without saying goodbye. Bill knew he was probably going to need a lot of help from his therapist to get back in good graces with Valerie.

Later that evening, Bill was sitting with his feet up on the edge of Ricky's desk waiting to see if there were any new developments, when Minsky barged in and said, "Why isn't his ass in a cell?"

"You haven't arrested him, yet," Ricky said. "I can't lock him up unless he's under arrest."

Minsky grabbed Bill by the collar and threw him up on the desk and flipped him over. He yanked Bill's hands behind him and cuffed him. "You're under the arrest for the rape and possible murder of Madison Porter."

"What?" Bill asked.

Ricky was on his feet. "Are you saying Madison has been murdered?" he asked. "If that's true, you know this man didn't do it."

As he read Bill his rights, tears filled Bill's eyes. Poor Madison. He didn't kill her with his own hands, but if she were dead, he was probably the reason she was dead.

"Where did you find the body?" Ricky asked.

"We haven't found the body, yet," the Ranger said.

"Then how the hell do you know she is dead?"

"We found her bloody clothes," Minsky said. "Her father identified them."

Bill sighed with relief and looked up at Ricky and smiled. Ricky was shaking his head. "Let the man go, you idiot," Ricky said. "Madison is a nudist. Why would she be wearing clothes?"

Minsky threw Bill back into his chair with his hands cuffed behind his back. Bill screamed out in pain as his hands were crushed.

"You should show me a little more respect, Sheriff," he said. "Seeing how I might be arresting you for aiding and abetting."

"With all due respect, sir, you are a major tool! If you'll sit down and tell us what's going on, we might be able to help you."

"What makes you think I need help?" Minsky asked.

"Well, for one thing, you are arresting a man for a murder he was supposed to have committed less than twenty-four hours ago who has been in my custody for more than twenty-four hours. And you're saying the only evidence you have is bloody clothing. Bloody clothing found at a nudist resort that belongs to a girl that is a nudist. You spent most of your time putting together a news conference, instead of going out and investigating the crime scene yourself. I'd say you need a lot of help."

The Texas Ranger looked pale. "You're the sheriff," he said, meekly. "Why didn't you go investigate the crime?"

"The warrant for his arrest was obtained through your office. I brought in the guy the warrant was for. He asked to be turned over to you. State jurisdiction trumps county, doesn't it?

It's your ball game."

He sat there in silence for a minute, and his face fell. "Hell, I'm so screwed," he said, softly.

Ricky laughed and said, "Yes, yes you are. Why not let me help you?"

The ranger nodded and asked, "What can you do to help?"

"First, let me take the cuffs off of Mr. Clark." Ricky said. "He's not going anywhere."

He pulled a key out of his shirt pocket and undid the cuffs, then handed them back to the ranger.

"Now, Bill, tell the ranger what happened."

Bill relayed the whole story. The Texas Ranger listened intently. "So, Miss Porter was alive when you left her," he asked, "and you think that she may still be alive?"

Bill sighed and said, "I hope so, but I'm pretty sure those bloody clothes are just a ruse to throw you off the scent. While you have all your manpower dragging the Frio, Whitman is getting away. What did Cathy Elkins tell you?"

"I haven't been able to find her."

Ricky looked at Bill with an alarmed expression. "She's probably in as much danger as Madison," he said. "I'm sure Whitman figured out who helped you escape."

Bill considered that for a moment and said, "Maybe, but it's also possible that I was allowed to escape. Whitman planned for me to get a lawyer and keep my mouth shut or come right out and try to implicate him. The fact that I didn't mention his name in the press conference caused him to seek another contingency plan. I wonder if any of those reporters have figured out who I was talking about, yet."

Ricky looked at his watch and said, "We've missed the news. We could find it on the internet, but I don't have internet here at the courthouse."

"Really?" Bill asked. "Why not?"

"The county commissioners thought it was a waste of money?"

"What about Chuck's computer?" I asked.

"That's an old mainframe computer for county records."

"The cost of operating that mainframe probably costs three times more than an internet connection," Bill said, with a laugh.

"More like ten times more, because we have to fly in a technician from Dallas every time it breaks down," Ricky said.

"And I thought Copper City was Hicksville," Bill said, shaking his head. "What about Cathy's computer?"

Ricky nodded and said, "I know where the extra key is. We can go look at it there."

They all stood, but Minsky said, "I'm sorry, Mr. Clark. I believe you, but you are still under arrest. I can't afford any more screw-ups. You'll need to stay here in the cell."

"I'm afraid I'm going to have to agree," Ricky said. "It would be hard to explain why I'm parading you over to an office building to surf the net."

Bill wasn't happy about it, but he knew they were right. "I understand. I'm a little tired anyway. Still if I'm asleep when you get back, wake me and let me know what is going on."

When the county jail door slammed shut behind him, he acknowledged the fear he had been feeling. If things didn't go well, this could really be his future. He prayed that Cathy and Madison were okay. Not only because he really cared about both of them, but also because they were the only ones who could get him out of this mess.

Bill hadn't really slept well since he arrived here. The cot in the cell wasn't comfortable at all. Out of pure exhaustion, he dozed off. He didn't know how long had been asleep when he was startled awake by footsteps outside the cell. He sat up to see who it was. He was expecting Ricky and Minsky, but to his horror he discovered it was Jerry Elkins.

Elkins unlocked the door and swung it open. Bill saw the .45 automatic in his hand. He was pointing it straight at Bill's head. "You screwed up, asshole," he said.

Bill closed his eyes and waited for the sound of his death.

CHAPTER 24

"Open your eyes," he said. "I'm not going to shoot you. At least, not yet. I just want you to come with me."

"I'd rather not," Bill said. "I'm under arrest. I don't want to get into any more trouble."

"I know this is hard to believe, seeing I have a powerful handgun pointed at your head, but if you don't come with me you won't live to see morning. There are very powerful bad guys on their way to off you. Cathy doesn't want that to happen. Personally, I don't give a shit. I'll count to three and then I'm shutting back the door. Your choice. One, two--"

Bill stood up and followed him out of the courthouse. They climbed into Elkins' Silverado pick-up and sped off to the edge of town.

"Where are we going?" Bill asked.

"Does it matter?"

"No, I guess not."

They rode in silence for a few miles. Jerry looked over at Bill and smiled. "I'm surprised you came with me. I really didn't expect you to," he said

"You didn't really give me much choice," Bill replied.

"Sure, I did."

"Yeah, but only three seconds to make it."

Jerry laughed.

"I just figured you've had multiple chances to kill me," Bill said, "and you hadn't done it, yet. So I suppose you don't really want to kill me."

"Really? How do you figure?"

"You could have shot me at the house in Forester, or when you blew my tires. And then when you zapped me with the stun gun."

Jerry laughed again. "I can see why Cathy likes you," he said. "You're a pretty smart fella."

"I also know that I've been played from day one by Cathy."

He frowned and said, "Yeah, dude. You're right about that. Welcome to the club. I'm impressed that you were able to resist her charms, though. Most other guys would have jumped right in bed with her."

"But I bet you've remained faithful to her just the same."

He turned and looked at Bill and said, "I still love her. No, I've not been with anyone else, but that hasn't been entirely by choice."

"She's only slept with other men to get what she wants," Bill said, sympathetically.

"I know, but that doesn't make me feel better."

"I'm sorry about your daughter," Bill said. "That must have been hard."

Jerry's eyes misted, but he quickly regained composure. "So, you know why this is happening. I'm sorry I can't talk about it. You got any kids?"

Bill shook his head and said, "Only an idiot wouldn't understand why you are going after Whitman. I'm sorry if I messed things up."

"Only for you, man," Jerry said. "I believe Cathy's plan is still on track. Once she wins, you may be okay, but she'll not let you get in the way. She does like you, though. Otherwise, she would have left you in that cell to die."

"Is Madison, okay?" Bill asked.

"I don't know. To be honest, I don't know if Cathy is okay. They are both with Whitman. Cathy sent me a text message to come get you. You might've exposed a little too much telling the press she took the picture. Other than that, I was impressed with the whole press conference thing. That was really clever. It wasn't what anyone expected. You threw everyone a curve ball, but especially Whitman. You have him rattled, which makes him all the more dangerous."

"Yeah, I didn't think about that."

They rode along in silence for a few more miles. It took Bill a little while, but he realized they were on the road to Forester. "Are you taking me back to Fifth Sun?"

He nodded.

"Isn't that place crawling with Texas Rangers?"

"You would think so, but it isn't. You'll be safe there."

"I was really enjoying being back in my clothes."

"That won't be an issue. You'll not be roaming around the resort."

Jerry pulled up to the resort and let Bill out at the gate. Jeremy Porter was waiting there in khaki shorts and a gray sweatshirt next to a Jeep. "Come with me," he said. Bill crawled into the passenger seat and someone opened the electric gates.

"I appreciate the help," Bill yelled over the whine of the jeep motor and the wind whipping around the topless vehicle.

"Don't thank me yet," Jeremy said. "This is purely for my own interests. If I need you for a trade for my daughter, I'll do it in a heartbeat."

"That's fair. I don't want anything to happen to

Madison, either."

Bill sat silently the rest of the way to the resort. Jeremy parked the jeep in front of his office and hopped out. "Follow me," he said, and Bill obeyed.

They went deep into the woods and Bill couldn't help thinking that this would be a good site for a shallow grave in which he would never be found. Suddenly, Jeremy stopped and reached down to the ground. He yanked open a camouflaged trap door and revealed a set of concrete stairs. "Go ahead. I'll turn on the lights after I shut the door."

Bill headed halfway down the stairs then stopped and looked up. Jeremy followed him and pulled the door shut. He heard a click and lights came on illuminating the stairwell. Jeremy pushed past Bill and said, "Down here."

At the bottom of the stairs, they came into a huge room, the size of a football field. It was filled with army-style bunk beds.

"Holy shit," Bill said.

"Pretty impressive, isn't it?"

"Seems a little much for a storm shelter."

He laughed and said, "This isn't a storm shelter. It's a bunker. My father had it built in 1993 after the Waco incident. He just figured it would be a matter of time before they came after us."

"How did he pay for it?"

"Texas taxpayers paid for it. I'm not sure how, but this was built from the funds and by the same contractor who built the underground extension of the state capital."

"There's an underground extension at the state capital?" Bill asked.

"Yep. Most of the taxpayers don't even know it's there. All this was happening while the world watched the standoff at

Waco. Sometimes the media can provide the smoke and mirrors for government magic."

"That's pretty cynical."

He smiled a tired smile, shrugged and said, "I suppose, but only if it isn't true. I'm not saying it was a conspiracy, but the lege benefitted from the distraction."

"And Whitman got this built under the table?"

"He got us the funds, but I don't know how."

"If he knows about it," Bill said. "Why won't he send his goons here?"

"I don't know how he would know you were here, but even if he suspected he would know that the security is too tight for him or his henchmen to breach. You'll be safe as long as you stay down here. I'm locking you in, and only I have the keycode."

"And if something happens to you, how do I get out?"

"There is a way, but I'm not going to tell you what it is," Jeremy said. "I'm trying to protect you, but I don't want you to get away."

"So, I'm your prisoner?"

"Yes, but it's better than jail. There's a big screen television and beer and food in the refrigerator, so you shouldn't be too bored. I'll check on you in the morning."

"Do you have a computer?"

"Yes, but don't check your emails. I'm sure our usage is being monitored."

"I just want to check the news," Bill said.

Jeremy looked at his watch. Bill couldn't help but notice how different he looked with his clothes on. "It's nearly midnight," he said. "Some of the San Antonio stations rebroadcast their ten o'clock report. I suggest you watch that. I have to go, though. These clothes are driving me nuts."

As Jeremy ascended the stairs Bill walked over to the huge flat screen television. He picked up the remote that looked like something from the cockpit of the space shuttle and found the power button on the LCD touch screen. Loud, crisp music surrounded him. He noticed a sound system that must have cost in the tens of thousands of dollars. Under other circumstances, he would have thought he'd died and gone to heaven.

The television was already tuned to CNN, but he hoped this story hadn't made national news. He was wrong.

"A New Mexico Journalist, suspected of child molestation and possibly murder, escaped from his Fayton County jail cell earlier this evening. A massive manhunt is searching for this man—"

"Great," Bill said out loud. They put up a picture that usually accompanies his editorials. Valerie said it made Bill look smarter than he was. Now, for the whole country that will be the picture in everyone's mind of what a sexual predator looks like.

"—Bill Clark, editor and publisher of the Copper City Daily Press, is believed to have molested a seventeen-year-old girl at a family nudist resort and some fear that he may have even taken her life. Clark implicated an anonymous politician in a press conference, but no discovery of that person's identity had been made. He admitted the sexual encounter—"

They showed a bite from Bill's press conference ".... I kissed her and she pressed her nude body up against me. I was about to have sex with her when someone snapped our picture..."

All Bill could think of at that moment was that he was glad both of his parents were dead.

"—Clark is believed to be armed and extremely dangerous," the reporter said, concluding the story."

"Armed! I'm not armed!" Bill shouted at the television.

He turned off the television and went to the

refrigerator. It was a huge stainless steel commercial refrigerator, and it was stocked with all kinds of food. One shelf was nothing but expensive imported beer. It was a temptation to just get really drunk, but he thought he'd better keep his wits about him. He needed some sleep. He decided he'd drink one beer and then crawl into one of the cots.

The leather couch in front of the television looked more comfortable than the bunk beds and it was in the darkest corner of the big room. He didn't think he wanted to turn out the lights. It would be way too dark.

The beer did the trick and Bill was able to get some sleep. He woke up because of his own snoring and checked his watch. It was seven in the morning.

He sat up and tried to focus for a few seconds. Despite expensive entertainment equipment and bright fluorescent lights, he felt overwhelmed by the silence. It felt as if he was in a crypt. To avoid panic he hit the power button on the remote. He needed some sound.

The president was speaking. Bill found comfort in the president's relaxed smile. The comfort was short-lived when the picture switched to a familiar face. One he'd seen just a few hours before. He turned up the volume and heard "—Jeremy Porter, owner of the nudist resort where journalist Bill Clark allegedly molested and murdered a girl was found at the bottom of the resort's pool. There was a single gunshot to the back of his head. The shot came from the same caliber of the gun Clark had stolen from the Sheriff's office.

"Oh, shit," Bill said.

CHAPTER 25

With Jeremy dead there was no way for anyone to get down there to Bill, but he also didn't know how to get out. He had enough food to last for a long time, but not forever. Surely someone knew how he could get out of there, but he only had one way to communicate with the outside world, and that was with the computer, but that might let the wrong person know his whereabouts.

What would they do if they found him? If they wanted to kill him it would be all too easy. They could cut off his air supply or gas him, and he would be buried in the world's biggest state-funded grave. They could even flood this place and drown him. Bill thought he'd rather be shot than suffocated or drowned. He needed to figure out how to get out of there.

Bill walked up the stairs and looked at the door. The locking system was electronic. He'd heard the buzz last night. It wouldn't have made sense that a person needed a keycode to get out. This was set up to keep people out, not in. Still, one needed to know how to open it and he didn't.

There was no button near the door, so he went back down the stairs and looked around the room. There were a few desks at the bottom. He got down on his knees and looked for a switch underneath the desks, but there was no wire leading to any of them. If Jeremiah had planned on some David Koresh-style standoff he wouldn't want to make it easy to open the door, but there had to be a switch or a button somewhere in the bunker.

Bill walked over to the desk with the computer and

turned on the CPU. As the monitor glowed, the program icons soon appeared. There was nothing to suggest that there might be a control for a door in any of the programs. There were a lot of games, which suggested that this computer was put down here primarily to entertain the kids. Jeremy wouldn't have any security programs here.

Panic was sitting in. Bill didn't know what was going on up above, but he didn't like sitting down there and waiting for death to come. He grabbed the remote and turned the television back on. Bill was dubious of television news and not just because he was a newspaper man. Twenty-four-hour news means that shortcuts have to be taken to keep the air filled. It means a lot of repetition of stating the obvious and tons of file footage. Every time there was a plane crash at sea, they would show the same footage of debris being pulled out of the water. No one watching had a problem with the fact that the debris was from a crash years ago. But if Bill had printed a picture of a car wreck from several years back to report a recent crash in the newspaper, his office would be flooded with calls.

To his regret, Fox news had dedicated an entire half-hour to his story. They were actually interviewing his third-grade teacher. "He was always a strange boy," she said. "I remember him peeing his pants several times."

This is relevant? The more he watched the story, the more he thought he'd be better off just dying in this stupid bunker. He looked down at the remote to change the channel and an icon caught his eye. It was marked "keypad." He tapped it and an alphanumeric keypad appeared, just like the buttons on a phone. Could this be it?

He stood up and walked back up the stairs. He tried punching in "M-A-D-I-S-O-N," thinking that if he were Jeremy that's the password he'd probably use. That didn't do anything. He feared that Jeremy had used a phone number or the last four digits of his social. If that were the case, he'd never get it. His only hope was if Jeremy was better at remembering words than numbers.

He thought for a moment what other words he might use. He punched in "N-U-D-E" and tried "N-A-K-E-D," but no luck. He tried several combinations of Fifth Sun, trying fifth, first, then sun, then both. Out of frustration he hit the number five and he heard the lock buzz. The number five! That was his password to open the door!

With the way things were going, he halfway expected to open the door and find an army of law enforcement people with their guns drawn. He cracked the door enough to peek out. There were four bare feet. The door flung open and there stood two naked people. It was Charlotte Brown and Chuck Tremaine.

"See," Charlotte said, "I told you he'd figure it out."

"I'm sure it was just dumb luck," Chuck said.

Chuck was absolutely right, but Bill still felt insulted. "What are you guys doing here?" Bill asked.

"Trying to save your ass," Chuck said.

"Take off your clothes," Charlotte said.

"I'd rather not."

"We need you to blend in," Charlotte said. "If you're wearing clothes the police will spot you right away. I have got to get you to my bungalow."

"I bet that's not the first time you've said that to a man," Chuck said.

"Probably less often than you, Chuck."

Naked, again, Bill followed Charlotte on the way to her bungalow. State troopers were everywhere. One of them headed in their direction. Chuck grabbed Bill by the arm and shoved him against the tree and started kissing him. He grabbed Bill's butt. The trooper clucked his tongue in disgust and turned away.

Chuck released Bill. Charlotte rolled her eyes. "You didn't have to grab his ass," she said.

"I know, but I wanted to."

They made it to Charlotte's bungalow. Bill sat on the edge of one of her beds and asked, "Now what?"

Chuck shrugged. "We figured you had a plan. Ricky just asked us to watch for when you came out of the bunker."

"Ricky knew where I was. He wasn't pissed that I escaped from his jail."

"Ricky understood, but Minsky is livid," Charlotte said. "He said if he catches up with you, he'll shoot you himself."

"Does he think I killed Jeremy?"

Chuck shook his head. "That ranger is a moron, but he knows that this whole mess is bigger than anything you could have done. Still, nothing points to Whitman except your word."

"Whitman is the one that killed Frankie," Bill said. "He told me himself."

"Then we got to figure out a way to get the bastard!" Chuck said, bitterly.

"I think Cathy is working on it, but I don't know what the plan is," Charlotte said.

Suddenly there was a huge explosion and the sky lit up with a giant orange ball of fire. Charlotte, Chuck, and Bill stared at the bright fire from the window. "What the hell was that?" Bill asked.

"That, my dear boy," said Charlotte, "was you being blown up in the bunker. At least, that's what someone was hoping for."

Bill sat back down on the bed and wondered if he looked as pale as he felt. "These people are pretty serious, aren't they?" he asked

"Well, this seems like a good time to go back to being an asshole," Chuck said. "I'm getting as far from you as possible."

Chuck was out the door before Bill could say anything, but he was actually glad to see him go. "You should do the same, Charlotte."

"I'm not afraid," she said. "I'm a librarian."

She didn't seem to be kidding. "Well, I don't want you getting hurt or killed for helping me, but I'm going to ask a big favor. May I borrow your car?"

"The keys are in my locker. I looked in your locker. Your clothes are still there, but no one seems to think there is a need to stake it out."

Bill wondered about Valerie. What if they had gotten to her? He thought about asking Charlotte if he could borrow her cell phone, but that would be dangerous for Charlotte. It would identify her as an accomplice. He had to get another phone somewhere.

Grabbing a towel from Charlotte's bathroom, he kissed her on the cheek and went outside. Cops were everywhere but they were mostly looking at the women and avoiding eye contact with the men. Bill walked over to the big pool, dropped the towel near the edge, and then dove into the water. It was freezing. Why wouldn't they heat both pools at a nudist resort?

Bill swam a couple of laps and stopped at the edge near the towel. He looked around to see if anyone was paying any attention to him. A couple of teenage girls walked by and all the men were watching them strut past them. Bill jumped out of the water and started drying his head as he walked towards the office. As far as he could tell he made it to the dressing rooms without being noticed. An elderly couple was undressing near him, but they didn't look up as he pulled Charlotte's car keys out of the locker.

As Charlotte had said, no one seemed to be watching his

locker. Bill grabbed his clothes, pulled them on, and ran out to Charlotte's car. It was stupid to run, and that was probably what caught a state trooper's attention. About a half-mile down the road, he noticed him in the rearview mirror. He turned on his lights. He continued until he got to the bump gate. He stopped as soon as the grill made contact with the gate.

The trooper pulled up right behind Bill, and Bill could see him speaking into his radio. The trooper stepped out of the car. He adjusted his hat and checked his reflection in the window of his cruiser. He strutted towards Charlotte's car without a care and confidence. Bill waited until the officer was almost to the back bumper and then took his foot off the brake and gunned the motor. The other side of the gate swung around and swatted the officer a good fifty feet into the field. He was still rolling when Bill looked in his mirror. The officer didn't move for a long time and Bill was afraid he might have killed him. Eventually the officer stirred, but Bill was over the hill, before he could see the man stagger back to his car.

Bill's hand was on the horn blaring all the way to the double gates and both were open when he reached them. He pulled in front of the store, stopped and ran inside. Pierced ear kid looked up. Bill had a hundred-dollar bill hidden in his shorts in an inside pocket. He pulled it out and put it in the kid's face.

"What's your name, Kid?" Bill asked.

"Craig," he said.

"Craig, this is yours if you'll shut the gates and not open them for twenty minutes for anyone."

"Hell, yeah," he said and took the bill.

There were some of those cheap prepaid cell phones behind the counter. Bill reached over and grabbed one. "Put it on Sen. Whitman's tab," Bill said.

"He doesn't have one," Craig said, "but it's cool. You can have it."

It wasn't easy trying to program the phone as Bill drove down the road at a hundred miles an hour, but he finally got it. Bill dialed Valerie's number and she answered.

"Are you okay?" Bill asked.

"I'm surrounded by a small army of local cops and feds, but otherwise I'm fine,"

"Where the hell are you?" She asked. "They told me they thought you were dead."

"Don't tell them otherwise," he said. "I'm in a car headed for Austin. I have an appointment with Senator Whitman."

"Does he know?"

"Not yet, but he will."

"Bill, no matter what happens—"

"I love you, too, Valerie," Bill said, then disconnected the call.

CHAPTER 26

There was really no reason for Whitman to be in Austin this time of year, but Bill assumed that he had a place to stay there. Whitman was not going to be taking Cathy and Madison to his home turf. Of course, Bill had no idea where Cathy and Madison were, or if they were still with the senator. He didn't want to muck up Cathy's plan further, but Jerry had made it pretty clear that Bill wasn't part of Cathy's plan. He intended to make himself a part of her plan whether she wanted him to be or not.

It was about four in the afternoon when he pulled into Austin. He'd had no lunch and was starving. He had not been to Austin often, but he had a friend there. He didn't know how she would feel about him after all this time, but he had looked her up on the computer a few years back. He knew where she lived.

The house in west Austin was a small mansion, but there was no security gate. Bill parked Charlotte's car in the big circular drive and walked to the front door. He rang the bell. The intercom speaker crackled, and a familiar voice said, "Yes. May I help you?"

"Emily?" Bill asked.

"Who is this?"

"It's Bill, Emily. Bill Clark."

The intercom went dead. Bill wondered what she was thinking. Did she know that the police were looking for him? As more time passed, he felt maybe he should get out of there. He turned to head for the car, when the front door opened and a woman in a colorful moo-moo sprang out wrapped him into a tight hug. "Oh my God, Bill. It's so great to see you," she said.

A moo-moo is what Bill's mother used to call a fat dress, but as he returned the hug, he realized that Emily must've been wearing it for comfort and not to hide fat. If anything, she was thinner than he remembered.

"I'm glad to see you, too, Emily, but I was afraid you'd still be angry with me,"z

She pulled away from him and looked him over. Gone was the long straight hair with the bangs, but otherwise she looked the same. "That was a long time ago, Bill. Honestly, I think your leaving me was the best thing that ever happened to me. I sobered up and got to work." She leaned over and kissed Bill hard on the lips. "Besides," she said, "I've had three husbands since you, so I save my anger for them. You still look hot. Are you still with Valerie?"

Bill smiled a flustered smile and said, "Yes, but it remains to be seen how long that will last."

"Yeah, I heard about you and the teenager," she said. "I guess you're still a fugitive."

Bill nodded

"You better park the car in the garage then." She stepped inside the door and grabbed a remote control. She pointed it at the garage and the door started to open. Bill got back in the car and parked it next to Emily's Cadillac Esplanade.

Bill followed Emily into her house and back to her huge kitchen. She asked him if he was hungry and pulled a delivery pizza box out of the refrigerator. "Do you want me to heat it up?" she asked.

"I like cold pizza and I really don't want to wait for it to heat. I'm starving," he said, as he grabbed a slice out of the box that she had laid on the huge island and took a seat on one of the barstools next to the island. She pulled out a couple Heinekens and handed Bill one. He took a huge bite of the pepperoni pizza and washed it down with the beer. Nothing ever tasted so good.

"So," she said. "What's going on?"

"It's a long story," Bill said. "Let me eat and you tell me what you've been up to these last twenty-something years. Then I'll catch you up on me."

"Okay. I finished a law degree and passed the bar. Spent a few years as a public defender, but I married the DA and had to quit. I started a private practice that is going well. Spend more time in divorce than criminal law these days. After dumping three husbands, I saw there was more money to be made in divorce. Occasionally, I'll defend a rich crook, but criminals make lousy clients."

"Even innocent ones?" Bill asked.

She smiled and said, "I saw the picture of you and that girl. You may not be guilty of a crime, but you're not completely innocent."

"So, you said you had three divorces?" Bill asked, redirecting the conversation.

"Yeah, I can pick a jury, but I can't pick a husband. I went from the DA to a film actor, and even a minister, but all three of them cheated on me. Why is that, Bill? What is it about me that causes men to find me so insufficient?"

Bill shrugged and swallowed more pizza and beer. "I don't know, Emily," he said, "but I can vouch for the fact that it had nothing to do with the sex. That was terrific. I just felt I had more in common with Valerie. And I didn't cheat on you. I just left you."

"Well, that may have been true for you, I suppose. After all, you didn't leave me for someone younger."

"Speaking of which," Bill said. "I didn't do anything with that girl. What you didn't see in the photograph was my hands in a set of handcuffs. The girl kissed me as part of an attempt to tarnish my reputation to deflect attention away from my murder. If that girl hadn't passed me the key with that kiss, I'd be dead."

"Who was going to kill you?"

"Senator Larry Whitman."

"Oh my god! He's the one you were talking about?"

Bill went on to tell her everything from the beginning. She pulled out a legal pad and took notes. It was amusing to see her put on the reading glasses. She caught his smile. "I just need them to see. We're getting old, Bill. But you have to admit, I still look pretty damn good."

"You look great," Bill said. "Do you think you could help me with this mess?"

"If you get arrested and avoid involuntary suicide while in jail, I can probably help you get a reasonable bail and provide you with a decent defense," she said. Him

"I don't think Whitman wants me to get to jail. I wasn't really asking for legal help, but that would be nice. I have a legal fund being built up for me back home, but I don't know how much that is. Right now, I just want to stay alive. That being said, I know I am probably putting you in danger right now. I shouldn't have come here, but you are the only person I know in this town."

She laughed and said, "You're in a lot of trouble if the only person you can trust is an ex-girlfriend that is now a divorce lawyer. But don't worry about the danger part. I've got friends that can make Whitman quiver in his boots. Unless, he hired some seriously stupid hit men, they won't come near here."

Bill didn't want to know whom she knew, but he suspected that she wouldn't offer that information anyway. Still, he believed her. "I want you to send a text message to Cathy from your cell phone. I can't send one from this cheap pre-paid phone."

Emily pulled out her cell. "Do you have her number?" she asked

Bill shook his head and said, "Can you look up the number on the Faytonville Gazette website? She has her cell number on there."

"Got it. I'm a little slow on the text messages. My niece could do it with both hands. I haven't figured that out. What do you want me to say?"

"Hey, Cathy. How's it going? I'm in Austin. How about getting a Corona?"

Emily laughed and punched in the message. "I had Coronas," she said, "You should have said something."

"The Heinekens are better. I'm hoping the Corona will act as a code word, so she'll know who it is."

In a moment, Emily's phone chimed. She picked it up and read the message. "It's says, Papadeaux's at seven-thirty."

"What's that?" I asked.

"Cajun seafood place on I-35, near 290 east," she replied.

"I will need you to go in and check it out for me," Bill said. "This could be a trap."

"I'd love to. I like Cajun food."

"Am I pushing it to ask you if you would wear something provocative?" Bill asked.

"That isn't the problem," Emily said, "but the opposite would have been."

Emily found shirt and nice slacks that one of her husbands had left behind. "Papadeaux's is not a fancy place, but you will stand out dressed as you are," she said. "You're a little smaller than Frank, but these should fit you well enough."

The clothes fit better than most the off the rack clothes healed and were certainly much nicer. He went commando because he couldn't bring himself to wear another man's briefs. He stepped out into the hallway after he dressed and twirled around for Emily's approval.

"Oooh, you look hot. Much better than Frank ever did. I'm beginning to regret letting you get away."

"You let Frank go, and he had much better taste in clothes than I do."

"Yeah, but you are much better than Frank without clothes."

"I'd argue that was a long time ago, but since you have seen a picture of me naked lately, I'll accept the compliment."

She laughed and said, "A lot of people have. I can't believe you went to a nudist resort."

"It was for a story."

She looked at her watch and said, "We've got time. You want to run out to Hippie Hollow?"

"Are you kidding? With clothes like this, I'll never be naked again."

They took Emily's Escalade to the restaurant. She parked in the parking lot of the hotel next to it. "Their lot is always too full," she said. "Besides you are probably safer here. I'll call you if the coast is clear. I don't know what Cathy looks like, but I certainly know Whitman. If I don't see Whitman, or someone I suspect is one of his thugs, you can come on in."

Emily was dressed to the nines. She was wearing a black cocktail dress cut down to her navel, and was just long enough to cover her behind him. She was certainly going to get a lot of attention. Bill imagined he could have walked in with her and no one, not even Whitman, would have noticed him.

Bill's cell rang and he answered. "Whitman's here," she said. "With a killer blond and your little girlfriend."

"Okay. Plan B then. I'll be right there."

Bill went around the back of the restaurant to avoid being seen too quickly. He peeked in the window and saw Emily at the bar. He was able to get to the bar without being seen by Whitman, who was sitting in a corner facing the door. Cathy and Madison were on each side and there was an empty chair at the table.

"Okay," he said, as he sat at the bar next to Emily. "Head for the bathroom and I'll follow behind. In that dress you're wearing there will be no men noticing me."

"You want me to flash Whitman a boob?"

Bill laughed and said, "I don't think that will be necessary, but I like the way you think."

She started to the bathroom with a strut so provocative that Bill was distracted as well, but he quickly fell in behind her and headed for Whitman's table. Whitman's eyes were focused on Emily and followed her all the way to the bathroom. When he turned back around, he gasped to see Bill at the table with him.

"Mr. Clark," he said. "I'm so glad to see you." Although, his expression showed that he was everything but.

"Before you try anything," Bill said, "You should know that I have a gun pointed at your groin. I don't imagine that shooting you would make my problems any worse. I'm sorry, Cathy, if this is interfering with your plan, but my staying out of it just wasn't working for me."

Of course, Bill didn't have a gun, but just hid his hands underneath the table.

"I know," Cathy said. "My plan hasn't been going too well, either."

"Now, now, my dear," Whitman said. "You're still alive for now. If your husband delivers the documents, then I let you live."

"So, you're holding these ladies hostage?" Bill asked.

"That's putting it rather crassly," the senator said, "I I prefer to consider them them as collateral. That sounds more businesslike, don't you think?"

"You plan to trade Cathy for the documentation she's acquired to put you away?" Bill said. "What about Madison?"

Whitman smiled. "I'm keeping her more for my own amusement. She's much too lovely to kill. Besides, I have her father as collateral."

Bill's eyes widened in surprise. "You haven't told her?"

"Told me what?" Madison asked.

"He's already killed your father," Bill said. "The news is saying that I did it, but it was his people, not me."

Tears filled Madison's eyes. She looked at Whitman with an expression of intense contempt. "You bastard!" she said.

"I'm afraid that we are going to have to terminate this meeting, Bill," Whitman said. "You are becoming a nuisance."

"If you are not careful," Bill said. "You'll find out how big of nuisance I can be. Cathy, when that lady in the black dress comes out of the bathroom, I want you and Madison to follow her to the car."

"What about you?" Cathy asked.

"I'll be right behind you."

Whitman laughed and asked, "Do you think I'm going to let them walk out?"

"You will if you don't want to be singing soprano."

Emily came out of the bathroom and Cathy and Madison stood. "Sit back down!" Whitman barked.

"Go now," Bill said.

"There's a little problem with your plan, Bill," Whitman said, and then pulled out a .38 revolver and aimed it at Bill's head. "Unlike you, I am not bluffing. I have a real gun."

CHAPTER 27

"Show me your hands," Whitman ordered.

Bill pulled out his hands and held them up. "Are you going to shoot me in front of all these witnesses?"

"Why not? You're a murderer on the run. I'll be a hero." He pulled back the hammer on the gun.

"No!" Cathy shouted and lunged for the gun. Whitman turned and shot her. Bill reached down, grabbed the edge of the table, and threw the table up into Whitman and pinned him to the wall. The gun fell to the floor and Madison picked it up.

Bill let the table go and Whitman saw the gun. His eyes widened and he threw his hands up in front of his face. "Please don't shoot me," he said with a quivering voice.

"To use your words," Madison said. "Why not?"

Bill bent down to check on Cathy. She was bleeding out of a wound in her side, but she was still breathing. "Emily, call an ambulance," Bill yelled.

"And then the coroner," Madison said. The coldness in her voice frightened Bill.

"Don't kill him, Madison," Bill said. "If you kill him, he'll miss out on all that's coming to him. It will be better if he stays alive and suffers."

"But he killed my father."

"I know, but don't kill him. It will just ruin the rest of your life"

She nodded and lowered her aim. The gun went off

loudly and all the other patrons, who were already hiding under tables screaming, were screaming louder, but those screams were drowned out by the screams of Whitman clutching his bleeding groin.

"Hand me the gun," Bill said. He took the gun, removed the remaining bullets and tossed the gun on the floor.

Soon the restaurant was filled with police and paramedics. They stood and watched as the other diners pointed at them and made statements. Soon, Madison and Bill were both cuffed and put in the same squad car.

"I wonder how long it will take them to realize that they just put a suspected rapist in the back seat with his victim," Bill said.

"I should be able to clear all that up," Madison replied. "Provided they will take the word of a seventeen-year-old that just shot the nuts off of a state senator."

"I'm afraid that picture will probably haunt me for the rest of my life," Bill said. "I'm sure it's posted all over the Internet by now."

"It'll be old news by next week," Madison said. "People will forget about it."

Bill nodded and said, "Most of them will, but I don't think my wife ever will."

"I'm sorry about that, but if you get divorced, look me up in a few years. Maybe we can finish what we started," she said, with a crooked smile.

"I'm hoping for something better for you, Madison. Somewhere there is a nice young man your age that will be lucky enough to win your favor. He better treat you right, or I will certainly look him up."

Before they could talk any further, someone yanked Bill out of the car. It was Minsky. "What the hell have you been up to?" he shouted.

"Hey, Minsky. Sorry to have run out on you, but I'm allergic to death."

"Don't be a smart ass," he said. "Tell me why I shouldn't shoot you myself."

"Because you'd miss my smile?"

"You can make jokes?" Minsky asked.

Bill frowned, shrugged and said, "What else can I do? How's Cathy?"

The Ranger shook his head and said, "She's still alive, but if the bullet hit any major organs she might be in trouble. There were a lot of witnesses that saw the senator shoot her, but he's arguing that he was trying to shoot you and she jumped in front of the gun. They have some security cameras, but they don't cover that area of the restaurant."

"Whitman's lawyers will probably make short work of those witnesses in court," Bill said. "He'll win if Jerry doesn't have the evidence of Whitman's past crimes."

Ricky walked up behind Bill. "Jerry doesn't have anything," he said. "He never did. It was a bluff. I don't know what Cathy's plan was, but it didn't work. Jerry said he thought you might be able to figure something out. He said you knew that he was the one who shot at us and blew your tires. How did you know?"

Bill shrugged. "I didn't really know," he said," but when he came and pulled me out of the cell things started to click. I saw you take the key with you when you left. Jerry had his own key to the cell. That's when I remembered that he was the curator of the museum and that he had access to all the previous sheriff's property, which probably included the spike strip and the stun gun. I also remembered that when we were being shot at, Cathy was uncharacteristically calm. I dismissed it as her just being a tough lady, which she is, but she was calm because she knew who was shooting."

Ricky frowned. "I'm going to need to have a little chat with Jerry when this is over. I think he needs to be relieved of his museum responsibilities."

The ambulances were gone, and the police were leaving. Bill saw the two men's eyes go wide when they turned to see Emily walking over. She looked a little shaken, but still stunning.

"Are you guys arresting my client?" she asked.

Minsky looked at Bill and asked, "This is your attorney, Clark? Jesus!"

"Gentlemen, this is Emily. Her last name used to be Peterson, but I suppose she's changed it a few times since. She's a good friend, but also an attorney."

"Actually, I never changed my name," she said. "I held on to mine. Saves me the trouble of changing all my papers every time I get married."

"Well, Ms. Peterson," Minsky said. "He was verbally arrested earlier, but he hasn't been arraigned. Actually, no paperwork has been done. I'd just as soon let him go for now."

Ricky nodded, and took out his key and removed Bill's cuffs.

"So, can we all go to the hospital and check on Cathy?" Bill asked.

The lawmen nodded in agreement.

"What about Madison?" Bill asked.

"She'll be taken to juvie," Emily said. "I'll go home and change clothes and see what I can do to get her released to my custody, but I doubt if they'll let me. She's a minor whose custodial parent has just been killed. It will take a lot of red tape. She could get charged as an adult, but the judge will be sympathetic."

"Her mother's still alive," Bill said.

"That will be the best bet," Emily said. "Do you know where I can find her?"

"She's at a nudist resort near Mineral Wells."

She shook her head. "All this nudity is going to give the media a hard-on. The conservatives will be yelling for someone to be hanged. I hope it's not Madison."

"Madison is a good kid," Bill said.

Emily smiled, sadly, and said, "I hope she can get through all this and stay that way."

When they got to the hospital, the nurses directed them to a surgical waiting room. They found Jerry sitting with his head in his hands.

"Hey, Jerry," Ricky said, softly. "How's she doing?"

He looked up at them and attempted to wipe away his tears. "The bullet punctured one of her lungs, but they think they can fix that. It would have gone all the way through, but it hit a rib. The doctors say she'll probably be okay, but they say it can go bad at any point."

"She's a tough lady," Bill said. "She'll be okay."

There really wasn't much else to say, so they just took a seat and waited.

Seven hours later, a very tired-looking doctor stepped into the waiting room. They all looked up. His expression wasn't encouraging.

"She lost a lot of blood," he said, "and she was deprived of oxygen for a while. I think she'll be okay, but we won't know for sure until she wakes up. It may be a long recovery, but she should be back to normal eventually."

Jerry looked relieved. "Can I be with her?" he asked.

"It'll be another thirty minutes, or so," the doctor said. "Once she gets settled in recovery, we'll come get you."

They sat in silence for a while, but Bill had to know something. "Jerry, tell me about your daughter."

Minsky clucked his tongue and said, "Can't you see what this man's going through?"

"I'm sorry," Bill said, "but I'm a reporter, not a minister. I need to know what happened."

"It's okay," Jerry said. "I want to talk about it. I think I need to talk about it."

He took a deep breath and sat up straight. "My parents were members of Jeremiah's cult. I left the cult as a teen. I got Cathy pregnant and married her. I'm fairly certain my parents kidnapped the baby. They thought I was going to hell, and they didn't want to lose their granddaughter to heretics. We tried everything to find her. Hired private detectives and pestered the local law. Cathy eventually seduced Ricky to get him involved, and he did all he could, but we never found our daughter. My parents died and never told me what happened."

"Whitman had to be mid-twenties at that point," Bill said.

Jerry nodded. "He had just won his first election to the Texas House of Representatives. My parents thought he was a god. Cathy knew what he was. She tried to tell others, but everyone in that cult knew Whitman was their bread and butter. No one would cross him.

"We'd been married five years when Cathy finally told me that Whitman had taken her virginity when she was twelve. I wanted to kill him right then, and now I wish I had, but Cathy convinced me that if I did, then we might never find our daughter.

"After Jeremiah died, Cathy joined the resort to try and find our daughter. Charlotte Brown had never been part of the cult. She had issues of her own, and she was sympathetic to us. She let us live in the basement of her house and helped us find jobs. I worked for the paper until the owner died. He was a widowed Jewish man with no children. He left the paper to me.

"There have been many girls that are the same age as what our Bethany would be. Cathy has had feelings about some of them, but she could never be sure. Some of those girls went missing. We knew it was possible that she was probably raped and killed by Whitman, but we've never been able to prove it."

A nurse came out and told Jerry that he could go be with his wife. "The rest of you can wait here if you like," she said, "but she'll probably not wake for another six hours, or so. She won't be able to have visitors until tomorrow morning."

As Ricky, Minksy, and Bill walked out of the hospital, Bill's cheap cell phone rang in his pocket. He answered it. It was Emily.

"I found the woman that you said was Madison's mother, and guess what, the mother was stunned to find out she had a daughter. She said she and Jeremy never had any kids."

Before he could respond, Bill lost the call because his prepaid minutes were up.

CHAPTER 28

Bill turned to Minsky and asked, "Do you think the Texas Rangers could help get a paternity test done."

"I'm not even sure I am a Texas Ranger anymore," he said. "I haven't checked in since you escaped. I'm sure there is some agency that could help, but it will require a bunch of paperwork."

"Speaking of checking in," Bill said. "Could I borrow your cell phone, Ricky?"

He handed it to Bill, and he dialed Valerie's number.

"Hello?" she said. Bill could hear apprehension in her voice.

"Valerie, it's me."

She let out a loud sigh. "Oh, thank God. What the hell is going on? The television says that girl shot Whitman. Is that true?"

"Yeah, but I don't know how he's doing. He shot Cathy, and she's in recovery. I'm at the hospital with the sheriff and a Texas Ranger. I'm okay."

"Are you going to prison?"

"That remains to be seen," Bill said, "but it's not a priority. I need some help on another matter. I'm going to give you the number of an old friend of ours — well, of mine. It's Emily. I want you to call her and she can fill you in."

"Emily! What the hell?"

"It's a long story. One I'll tell you when I get more time. I need you to just trust me on this."

OTHA FOSTER

"Okay," she said. "What's the number?"

Bill gave her the number, said goodbye, and handed the phone back to Ricky. "Can we go get something to eat?" Bill asked.

"Where do you want to eat?" Minsky asked.

"Anywhere besides Papadeaux's" Bill said.

They found a burrito place that wasn't too bad and drove back to the hospital parking garage. Bill attempted to sleep in the Ricky's squad car. Since he was still the prisoner, technically, he got the whole back seat to himself. The smell was terrible, but he managed to get a few winks.

He woke up when he heard Ricky's cell phone ring. Ricky answered it. "Yeah," he said. "We'll be right up." Ricky closed the call and turned back to Bill and said, "Cathy's awake. Let's go."

They walked into the hospital and took the elevator to the floor where they were told Cathy was. The nurse met them at the door. "You can go in," she said, "but don't ask her a bunch of questions. She needs to rest."

Cathy smiled when they walked in. She looked awful, but not that bad considering all she'd been through. "What happened to Larry?" she asked with a raspy whisper.

"Madison shot him in the nuts," Ricky said.

Cathy started to laugh, but then winced in pain. "Is he going to go to jail?" she asked.

"I don't think so," Bill said. "Not unless something new comes up."

"Check his computer. The one at his condo here in Austin."

Ricky looked at Minsky. "There's enough for probable

188

cause," he said. "A Texas Ranger could get that warrant."

"I'll see what I can do," Minsky said and pulled out his cell phone and walked out of the room.

"Madison?" Cathy asked. Her voice was getting weaker.

"Cathy," Bill said. "Madison is fine. You get some rest. Jerry, I need you to go to the lab here and give them a sample for a paternity test. It's longshot, but I think I know who your daughter is."

Emily was able to get the results expedited. She called Bill.

"Was I right?" Bill asked.

"Yes. It usually takes two days to get the results, but I threatened them with everything legal I could think of. You want to go with me and get their daughter out of juvie? Are you going to tell them, or do you want to surprise them?"

"Let's surprise them."

Ricky did not protest when Bill asked if he could go with Emily to pick up Madison. Emily was waiting for him downstairs. When they got to the juvenile detention facility, the receptionist informed Bill and Emily that it would take couple of days to arrange for Madison's release. Emily pulled out her cell phone and made a quick call. Five minutes later, a very pale looking man appeared with Madison who was wearing a pink jumpsuit two sizes too big. The man instructed the receptionist to give Madison back her street clothes. Madison changed back into the dress she had been wearing when she was arrested. They were soon driving back to the hospital.

"Who did you call?" Bill asked.

"The governor," Emily said. "He and I once had, shall I say, an evening together. That is all I am going to say."

Bill understood.

Everyone was pleasantly surprised when Bill and Emily

walked into Cathy's hospital room with Madison. They were happy to see Madison, but then Bill said, "Madison, go give your mother a hug."

They stood there staring at Bill for a long time as what he said sunk in. Bill just grinned as tears formed in all their eyes, and Madison walked over and took Cathy into an embrace. Jerry joined them and were soon sobbing in a group hug. Bill signaled to Emily for them to leave. This was a family thing.

As they walked down the hall Emily said, "Everything else could go to shit today, and this would still be the best day I ever had." Bill agreed.

Things didn't go to shit though, at least, not right away. They met Ricky in the lobby, and he was on the phone with Minsky. He listened intently to what the man had to say. "Okay. Thanks, Ben," Ricky said, and ended the call. Bill had rarely seen Ricky smile, but now he had a broad grin on his face.

"What did he say?" Bill asked.

"They found a whole bunch of nude photos of Madison on Whitman's computer. She was in a lot of lewd poses. Enough to nail Whitman for kiddie porn. Minsky thinks Madison and Cathy took the pictures and put them on his computer while he had them there as prisoners, but it won't make any difference. Just the mention of kiddie porn to the press and that man's career is over."

"But I still have money!" said a man from behind us. They turned and saw Whitman in a wheelchair. Behind him stood a large ugly man with his hand on a gun he had tucked in his belt. "Enough money to pay this man to kill all three of you with only one witness—me."

CHAPTER 29

"You expect to get away with this?" Ricky asked.

"Not really," Whitman said, "but that's not really my objective. It's possible for me to manipulate the media enough to fix all this, but I don't really care. The process will be more enjoyable knowing that the people who caused all this are dead."

"I take it the prognosis for your future sex life is rather grim." Bill said.

"I'm impressed, Mr. Clark. You're about to die and you bring up one of the main reasons I wanted to kill you. Yes, Madison was a good shot. The damage is permanent."

"She's a lot like her mother," Bill said.

Despite his obvious evil intentions, Whitman looked like a rather small pathetic old man in that wheelchair with all the tubes attached. When what Bill said sunk in, he looked even smaller. His face fell. "So, she knows," he said. "That's unfortunate."

"She also knows what you did to her mother," Emily said.

"I guess I should have let her kill you when she had the chance," Bill said.

"This conversation has lost my interest. I would prefer to kill the sheriff in more subtle ways, as I did Sheriff Prine and Deputy Elkins, but that isn't expedient," Whitman said, and turned to the ugly man. "Shoot the sheriff first."

Ricky smiled. "It's too late for that," he said. "He must be from up north."

"Why do you say that?" the big man asked.

"Because your gun is still in your belt and you think you can outdraw a Texas sheriff."

The big man's eyes widened, and he pulled his gun out of his belt, but Ricky already had his gun out and shot the man between his eyes. The big man crashed to the floor. Whitman fell out of his chair and grabbed the man's gun. He lifted the gun and aimed it at Ricky. Ricky said, "Thanks," and fired. Whitman's chest exploded and he collapsed into a lifeless lump on the floor.

The bell on the elevator rang. Ricky wheeled and aimed the gun in that direction, but quickly dropped it down when he saw Valerie exit the elevator. She looked around and said, "What the hell?"

Bill was elated to see Valerie, but a little shaken thinking of what could have happened if she'd appeared a few seconds earlier. Bill stood and walked over to her and took her into an embrace. "I'm really glad you're here," he said. "I've had a really bad week."

On television cop shows, this would have been the part where the police would have come in and taken statements and told people not to leave town. It's just not that simple in real life. A Texas state senator had just been killed and rumored to be involved in a sex scandal. This wasn't going to be cleared up in a few days.

The first shock Bill would discover was that there were a lot of people who were really angry. The second shock was most of them were angry at him. It seemed that most of the people in Texas wished he'd been the one shot, and not Whitman.

Thirty-five years in state government gives a person

a lot of power—power Whitman didn't acquire by himself. Whitman, no doubt, made a lot of deals that were less than kosher. If his life was opened up to a criminal investigation his secrets were in danger of being exposed. Many of the local judges got their appointments with Whitman's help. None of them were eager to hear Bill's side of the story. Bill was quickly arrested and thrown in a cell.

While trapped in that cell, the media were allowed to stand outside and pepper him with questions. Apparently, none of them had ever figured out that it was Whitman he was trying to implicate in the press conference. They acted as if Bill had done them some personal injustice.

"Mr. Clark, why didn't you tell us it was Whitman that had steered you to the nudist resort?"

Emily had told him not to speak to the press, so he said, "No comment."

"You might as well answer our questions," one reporter said. "You've nowhere to go, and we're not leaving without a quote."

"Okay," Bill said. "Here's a quote: the fact that none of you could figure out that I was talking about Whitman means you were either too lazy to go check the facts or too stupid to find them."

Bill didn't read or watch any of the news reports, but he imagined that they didn't quote him.

They kept him locked up for three days with no visitors. Eventually, Emily and Valerie were allowed to visit.

"I'm sorry, Bill," Emily said. "I called everyone I know, and no one will return my calls. Everyone is too busy working on damage control. They're all scrambling to cover their asses. Whitman had a finger in everyone's pie."

OTHA FOSTER

Bill laughed. "Am I an enemy combatant?"

"If you were," Valerie said, "we could help you. As far as the judges here are concerned you don't even exist. If they could figure out how to make that true, they would."

"How is everyone else doing?" Bill asked.

"Ricky was sent home and told to keep his mouth shut," Emily said. "Wisely, he went to the hospital security and had the video footage copied to his computer before the police arrived. It was a clean kill, and they know it."

"What about Whitman's computer?"

"That's a funny story," Valerie said, "but I doubt if you'll laugh. Minksy was called to testify at a senate hearing committee. He was hailed as a hero and even given a standing ovation. However, when he got back to his office, he'd found that someone had broken in and stolen Whitman's computer."

Bill did laugh. "You're right, that is funny. How's Cathy?"

"She's fine," Emily said. "They're all back in Faytonville as a big happy family. The juvie judge tried to lock Madison back up, but I reminded him that I knew where he lived, and I'd come over and do to him what Madison did to Whitman."

Bill sighed. "Well, that's good news. Do you think I'm going to end up as an involuntary suicide?"

"No," Emily said. "They just want you to disappear quietly. They've held you as long as they can. They're about to release you. You're booked on the earliest possible flight to El Paso, and they will probably escort you to the New Mexico border."

Bill looked at Valerie and said, "Well, I hate to disappoint them, but I'm not going home, yet."

"Why not?" Emily asked. "I thought you'd be dying to leave."

"I still haven't got what I came here to get."

Valerie nodded. "Your mother. You want me to stay here with you?"

Bill shook his head. "No, you need to get back, and I think this is something I need to do alone."

They did release Bill just as Emily said they would, and the police were unhappy to hear that he wasn't leaving the state right away. Emily loaned him her car to drive back to Faytonville. He considered going to talk to Ricky's mother, but he decided that would just cause unnecessary delay in the inevitable.

He drove to the library, and Charlotte looked up at him in surprise as he walked in. This time she was wearing the glasses on a chain. He walked over to her and said, "Mom, can we talk?"

Her eyes misted immediately, fogging up her glasses, and she pulled them off and let them hang by the chain around her neck. She reached for a tissue and began dabbing her eyes, and then blowing her nose. "How long have you known?" she asked, finally.

"I'm pretty sure I knew it the first time I saw you. I don't think a boy ever fails to recognize his mother no matter how many years they been apart."

"Why didn't you say anything?" she asked

Now the tears formed in Bill's eyes. He said, choking back a sob, "It seems that you went to hell of a lot of trouble to separate your life from mine, and it seemed you're willing to go to even more trouble to keep separated from me. Hell, you took your own son to a nudist resort without flinching."

She laughed. "Yeah, well, I've been a nudist for a while

now, so I pretty much embraced the lifestyle, so it probably didn't seem as awkward to me as it did you."

"That explains that, but it doesn't explain everything else," Bill said.

"Let's go to my house and let me explain it all over dinner. I owe you an explanation and a whole bunch of dinners."

Bill followed Charlotte to her house. It was small and modest with clapboard siding and a little picket fence. It reminded him of his maternal grandparent's home is Rising Star. It struck him as sad knowing that the nice old couple, who'd bought him his first stick horse, were now long dead without him ever getting to see them again. He wondered how they had felt about the separation.

Charlotte asked Bill if he'd like a beer, and Bill nodded. She pulled out a can of Lone Star from the refrigerator, grabbed a glass from the cabinet, and handed both to Bill. She motioned him to a red-topped stainless-steel dinette set and told him to take a seat.

"This looks like the dinette set we had in our kitchen in Forester," Bill said.

"It is, and the couch in the living room was the one we were sitting on the night Teresa fell on our porch, though it's been reupholstered a few times. I don't hang on to my family very well, but I do hang on to possessions."

Bill saw her eyes mist and realized that the possessions might have been an attempt to hold on to the past some, but he wasn't a shrink. He wasn't anywhere near ready to start empathizing with this lady, yet.

"What happened to Papaw and Meemaw?" Bill asked, wincing at the childish name that he'd known them by.

"Actually, they were killed in a car wreck in Houston. They were run over by an 18-wheeler on I-10. They really missed you. I don't think they ever forgave me losing contact with you."

Bill took a sip of his Lone Star. "So," he said, "Why did you lose contact with me?"

She nodded. "Let me get this chicken cooking, and I'll try to tell you. It won't be a very satisfying explanation, but it will be the truth."

"That's all I ask for."

She began cutting a whole chicken into pieces. Bill had never learned to do that. He always bought his chickens cut up. He had a déjà vu experience watching her and knew that he must have played this scene before. With remarkable speed she soon had the chicken frying on the stove.

Charlotte grabbed another beer out of the refrigerator, popped the top, and took a swig out of the can. "I'm not going to mince words, Bill. The problem was I was spoiled, stubborn, and pig-headed. I was used to getting my way, and for most of my marriage to your father he let me have my way. My mistake was that I took his amazing patience for weakness, and I resented him for his weakness. Finally, however, he surprised the hell out of me when I came home to find that he had a line I couldn't cross. He was okay with a lot of my shit, but there was a limit."

"What did you do to cross that line?"

"I tried to help Teresa by getting the goods on Whitman, which I never could, but I became Cathy's father's confidential informant. It required me to infiltrate Fifth Sun, which meant I had to become a nudist."

Bill nodded. "I suppose that was quite a shock to my Southern Baptist father."

"Shock doesn't describe it. At the time, your father was a fundamentalist minister that thought all the world's problems lay in the sin of co-ed swimming. He called it 'mixed bathing.' When he heard that not only were Fifth Sun people swimming together, but doing it nude in the name of religion, he put all his church's resources behind battling them. When I joined them, he went ballistic. You don't remember?"

The question stunned him. No, he didn't remember, and then, slowly the images started coming. He was standing in the doorway of his parent's bedroom. His father was screaming. He'd never seen him so angry. He couldn't make out the words his father was saying, but he was terrified at the expression on his father's face. "He-he was pointing a gun at you."

Charlotte nodded. "I was certain he was going to shoot me. He kept calling me a whore, and said he had a right to shoot me."

"He kicked you out of the house."

"Yes, but do you remember what he did just before."

This was it. This is what he'd been repressing. He didn't want to remember it, but it was coming. "He made you take off your clothes," Bill said.

"That wasn't all, was it?"

Bill began to tremble. Tears streamed down his face. "H-he raped you. With me watching. I remember. He knew I was watching, and he kept yelling at you, and at me. He said, 'This is what you do to whores, Billy Boy!'"

Charlotte was sobbing now. "I begged him to stop, and at some point, he seemed to realize what he was doing. He stopped and ordered me out of the house. He didn't allow me any clothes but said the town should see my shame. I left, grabbed a sheet off the clothesline, and went to the neighbors."

"You left me with that monster," Bill said.

She smiled through her tears. "You know he wasn't a monster. He was a kind, sensitive man that got pushed too far. He was a good father to you, wasn't he? Other than this one mistake, you know he was a good man."

Bill nodded. "Yes, he was. That is probably why I repressed the memory. He was a good father, but why didn't you fight for custody? Why did you desert me?"

"Things were different back then. I didn't have any money, and your father was well respected. I was the nudist, and there weren't many open-minded people back then. Not in these parts. Besides, I didn't really think I'd be a good mother."

"So, you really didn't do the nudist thing just to help Teresa, did you?"

She stared down into the frying pan, watching the grease bubble. Bill was afraid that he'd touched a raw nerve, but she didn't seem to be stinging in any way. She was lost in thought. "No," she said, finally. "I did it for me. I just used her as my excuse."

The reporter side of Bill ran questions through his mind, but he didn't ask them. The little boy watching his mother fry chicken was starting to take over. "Why? What was it you needed that caused you to leave your child behind?"

She looked up surprised. "Oh, please believe me that if I had it all over to do again, I would never have left you. I never intended to do that in the first place."

"Then why didn't you come find me when I got older? I could have spoken up and the judge would have listened. I could have come and lived with you."

"I did find you."

This stunned Bill. "What do you mean?"

"That's not really true," she said. "I never really lost you. Your Aunt Betty kept me posted. I was at most of your Little League games, even though you sucked at baseball. I was at both of your graduations, and I would have been at your wedding if it had not been that small hippie ceremony you decided to have. There was no way for me to crash that anonymously. I was also at your father's funeral."

"Why didn't you tell me?"

"Because you were doing just fine without me. I thought your father was a pacifistic loser, but he was a good father, and your stepmother was a good lady who did as good a job as I would have. You didn't need a mother who liked to hang out naked with strangers."

"Except I turned out to be an obsessive jealous husband with abandonment issues."

She laughed. "That sounds like a bunch of psycho-bullshit. You're just a typical average guy, who married way above himself, and it's normal to feel jealous."

Bill thought about the fact that the whole reason he'd come was because his therapist told him that his mother's desertion was the core of his problems but realized that his mother was probably right."

She turned off the stove and scooped out the chicken onto a plate. She sat it down in front of Bill and asked, "You still like the legs?"

Bill did, and he devoured one. They visited late into the night, and he spent the rest of the night in her spare bedroom. The next morning Bill got up and drove back to Austin and caught a flight home. Nothing had really changed, and everything had changed. Bill made one major decision, however. He wasn't going back to that therapist.

Unfortunately, Jeremy died before he could explain his part in the kidnapping of Madison. He was buried with a little ceremony, but Madison grieved the death of this man who raised her as his father. In the end he acted as an advocate, so no one felt the need to say anything negative about him. Had he lived he would have been held accountable for being part of the conspiracy to kidnap Cathy and Jerry's child.

Bill understood too well the adjustment Madison was going through. There was a sense of family connection, but the years separated still made them strangers. Madison had never known that Jeremy was not her father, so she had no repressed anger towards the Elkins. She told Bill that she knew she should be angry with Jeremy, but he had been a good father and had protected her from Whitman. No doubt she was kidnapped to be raised and later groomed by Whitman, but why would Jeremy participate in the kidnapping, but draw the line at abuse?

For all practical purposes, the Elkins would forever be Madison's adult friends. She lived with them one year, and then went to college. Bill's mother, Charlotte and Chuck Tremaine managed the resort while Madison was away at school, but when Madison finished, she returned to run the resort herself. She said she could never really adjust to the textile world.

No charges were ever filed against Bill Clark. There was a lot of yelling and screaming; some finger-pointing and threatening, but the truth finally won out. The cop Bill swatted with the bump gate could have filed charges, but Bill figured the officer was too embarrassed to report it. Finally, every state official involved recommended that Bill go back to New Mexico and stay there, which he gladly did. Valerie met him at the airport in El Paso.

Bill threw his suitcase in the bed of his pickup, and he started for the passenger door, but Valerie jumped out and told him to drive. Valerie hated driving in El Paso. Bill gave her a kiss when she crawled back into the truck and said, "It's good to be back."

"You gonna start walking around naked now?" Valerie asked.

"Nope," he replied. "I think the people who came up with clothes had the right idea."

"Do you think all your demons have been exorcised?"

"Only time will tell, but I don't think it'll hurt to keep a couple of them around for company, if nothing else."

OTHA FOSTER

Made in the USA
Coppell, TX
30 January 2024

27901281R00122